NOTES FROM UNDERGROUND

Notes from Underground

FYODOR DOSTOEVSKY

Translated by

Boris Jakim

WILLIAM B. EERDMANS PUBLISHING COMPANY

GRAND RAPIDS, MICHIGAN / CAMBRIDGE, U.K.

Originally published 1864 in Russian
under the title *Zapiski iz podpolya*

English translation © 2009 William B. Eerdmans Publishing Co.

Published 2009 by
Wm. B. Eerdmans Publishing Co.
2140 Oak Industrial Drive N.E., Grand Rapids, Michigan 49505 /
P.O. Box 163, Cambridge CB3 9PU U.K.

Printed in the United States of America

14 13 12 11 10 09   7 6 5 4 3 2 1

Library of Congress Cataloging-in-Publication Data

Dostoyevsky, Fyodor, 1821-1881.
[Zapiski iz podpolya. English]
Notes from underground / Fyodor Dostoevsky; translated by Boris Jakim.
p.   cm.
ISBN 978-0-8028-4570-2 (alk. paper)
1. Russia — History — 1801-1917 — Fiction.
2. Russia — Officials and employees — Fiction.
I. Jakim, Boris.   II. Title.

PG3326.Z4   2009
891.73'3 — dc22

2009006929

www.eerdmans.com

Contents

Dostoevsky's Wager

Robert Bird

Upon his return to St. Petersburg at the end of 1859, thirty-eight-year-old Fyodor Dostoevsky threw himself into public life with an impatience fueled by ten years of remote isolation. After being convicted of participating in a seditious conspiracy in December 1849, he had spent four years in an Omsk prison-camp and then almost six more in compulsory military service in Semipalatinsk (now Semei, Kazakhstan). Long before his arrival in the capital, Dostoevsky had feverishly begun to follow intellectual news and to correspond with leading literary figures, including his former co-conspirator, Aleksei Pleshcheev, and future rival Ivan Turgenev. He had also started publishing eagerly anticipated new works — namely, the story "Uncle's Dream" and the novel *The Village Stepanchikovo and Its Inhabitants* — which hearkened back to the styles and concerns of the 1840s. Despite the goodwill shown to their author upon his return from the ranks of the living dead, the cool critical reception of these first new works showed that Dostoevsky had much catching up to do. Upon reaching St. Petersburg, Dostoevsky set out to meet old friends and new literary stars alike, including Turgenev, poet Iakov Polonsky, and Nikolai Chernyshevsky. Two volumes of his collected works were published in Moscow at the start of 1860. Though still banned from occupying such posts officially, Dostoevsky also became de facto co-editor of his brother Mikhail's intellectual review *Vremia (Time)*, which began appearing as a monthly in January 1861. Within a year he was well on his way to reclaiming the all-too-brief fame he had enjoyed prior to his arrest in April 1849.

In addition to his purely literary ambitions, however, Dostoevsky was also driven by a higher purpose, acquired during his time in the prison camp, where he had owned only a single book: the Gospels. Though he had never been hostile to religion, he now seemed intent on remaking his art in the light of his renewed beliefs, not just in its subject matter but also in its very shape. Instead of simply resuming his original career path, Dostoevsky would allow his unplanned detour to Siberia to lead him in a wholly new direction. Instead of becoming a writer in the literary establishment, he would undertake to redefine literature as such. The crucial decision was to cease projecting ideas onto fictional forms and to allow both form and idea to emerge viscerally from his raw experience. Ceding a degree of control over his own imagination, Dostoevsky entered into a kind of wager on form, trusting that it would overcome the unsightliness of his times and milieux.

Even as he left Siberia, he began planning a new work, *Notes from the Dead House*, in an utterly original style. He described it in a letter he wrote to his brother on 9 October 1859:

> My personality will disappear. They are the notes of an unknown man; but I guarantee they will be interesting. There will be the most capital interest. They will be serious, gloomy, humorous, and colloquial conversation in the prison style [. . .] and the representation of people about whom literature has never even heard; they will be touching and, finally, most importantly, they will bear my name.[1]

Notes from the Dead House is justly regarded as the first great work in the Russian literature of captivity after Archpriest Avvakum's autobiography from the 1670s. Like Avvakum in his *Life* and like Aleksandr Solzhenitsyn in his "experiment in literary investigation," *The Gulag Ar-*

---

1. F. M. Dostoevskii, *Polnoe sobranie sochinenii* (Moscow, Leningrad: Nauka, 1972-1990), vol. 28-1, p. 349. Further citations of this edition will be given parenthetically in the text.

chipelago (1973), Dostoevsky found himself obliged to invent a new literary form for a world that refused to submit to conventional means of literary representation. Instead of an authoritative narrator, Dostoevsky entrusted the work to the eccentric Aleksandr Petrovich Gorianchikov, a former inmate whose "notes" have allegedly been recovered and published by an unnamed editor. Instead of following a linear structure, Gorianchikov's *Notes* document stories he overhears from his fellow inmates and then provide a thematic analysis of life in the Siberian prison camp. Throughout the work, the reader is reminded of the impossibility of conveying even a fraction of the visceral experience in conventional literary form. At the same time that he was reinstating his name in the media culture of his day, Dostoevsky was undertaking its fundamental analysis and critique.

Along with his vibrant, even racy language (which Boris Jakim has captured in his new translation), Dostoevsky's visceral experimentalism is a major reason why, almost a hundred and fifty years later, the texts he produced from 1860 to his death in 1881 retain such freshness and energy. Of course, despite the obvious differences, the overall contours of our ideological and cultural world have remained remarkably stable over this time. Just as Nietzsche seems far closer to us than to Hegel, so also Dostoevsky anticipated our concerns and, in crucial respects, has continued to shape our attitudes more than many of his greatest contemporaries. As with Nietzsche, the intricate and provocative form of Dostoevsky's texts has thus far resisted domestication in our media-saturated world. Though classic in the permanency of the claims they make on readers, Dostoevsky's works help each new generation of readers to discover their own opaque undergrounds and invisible skyways.

Written "deep in the shadow of the dead house,"[2] *Notes from Underground* was another wager on form. As the specific ideological context has receded from view and mass-media culture has become ever more pervasive, the formal provocation of *Notes from Underground* has increasingly become the site of contention. In addition to appreciating its

2. Robert Louis Jackson, *The Art of Dostoevsky: Deliriums and Nocturnes* (Princeton: Princeton University Press, 1981), p. 170.

biographical and ideological contexts, it is important to understand why *Notes from Underground* took the form that it did and how this form continues to affect our reading of it.

Ideology and Fiction

The year 1860 was an auspicious moment for Dostoevsky to join the journalistic fray. Since the death of Nicholas I in 1855, Alexander II had led Russia on a long-overdue series of reforms, resulting in the emancipation of the peasantry from serfdom on 19 February 1861. Part of the reform process was the gradual loosening of restrictions on education and the media known as *glasnost'*, which released much pent-up creative energy and quickly ushered in the major elements of a civil society. Alongside his fictional works, Dostoevsky continually worked on the journal *Vremia,* both as author and as editor. Most notably, after traveling in Western Europe from 7 June to 23 August 1862, Dostoevsky wrote his *Winter Notes on Summer Impressions,* his most sustained piece of social commentary from the 1860s, which amounted to a thorough and impassioned attack on the foundations of modern society as exemplified by Britain, France, and Germany.

Meanwhile, writing from the prison cell he had occupied since July 1862, Nikolai Chernyshevsky (1828-1889) was publishing his subversive novel *What Is to Be Done?* in the rival journal *Sovremennik (The Contemporary).* This was a major oversight on the part of the censors, because *What Is to Be Done?* was written and read as a transparent program for the radical reformation of Russian society under the leadership of heroic individuals of iron will. The views that brought Chernyshevsky to this vision were close to utilitarianism, meaning that actions should be judged in terms of their expediency. Naturally, utilitarians assumed that we can know the standard against which expediency can be measured; usually it was economic well-being. In Chernyshevsky's rational egotism, utilitarianism as a method coincided with socialism as a goal: in essence, it is in everyone's individual self-interest that the whole of society flourish. Chernyshevsky's novel implied revolutionary action as a means of establishing this self-evident truth.

Appearing at the same time, Dostoevsky's *Winter Notes* share major concerns with Chernyshevsky's novel, albeit viewed from the opposite end of the political spectrum. Both works feature the image of the Crystal Palace, a vast iron-and-glass structure created in London for the 1851 World's Fair and left standing for twenty-five years afterwards as a museum of — and monument to — the aspirations and power of modernity. In Chernyshevsky's work, the Crystal Palace appears in the heroine Vera Pavlovna's "fourth dream" as the home for inhabitants of a future paradise of joyful labor and abundant, equal rewards; both the natural landscape and the social structure have been transformed after everyone suddenly realized that they should strive for "what is useful": "It is only necessary to be cautious, to be able to organize well and to learn how to use resources to the greatest advantage," explains Vera Pavlovna's Vergil. Dostoevsky's response to the Crystal Palace was quite different. He saw it not as a prototype for thoroughly rational society but as a delusion of human grandeur that merely accentuated the contrast between human aspiration toward an ideal and the sordid street life of the modern city:

> It is a kind of biblical scene, something about Babylon, a kind of prophecy from the Apocalypse fulfilled before your very eyes. You feel that it would require a great deal of eternal spiritual resistance and denial not to succumb, not to surrender to the impression, not to bow down to fact, and not to idolize Baal, that is, not to accept what exists as your ideal. . . .[3]

For Dostoevsky, Chernyshevsky's novel was not merely a mistaken ideology; it signaled a failure to hold society to the highest moral standard — that of Christianity — and therefore a fatal compromise with conscience.

3. Fyodor Dostoevsky, *Winter Notes on Summer Impressions*, trans. David Patterson (Evanston, Ill.: Northwestern University Press, 1988).

In crucial respects, *Notes from Underground* represents the culmination of the ideological duel between Dostoevsky and Chernyshevsky. For one thing, it features the image of the Crystal Palace, which the Underground Man assails as a prison-house of the human will. In the Underground Man's thorough critique of Chernyshevsky's utilitarianism, one senses Dostoevsky's own outrage at the replacement of morality with a form of economic calculation, which for him was an offensively reductive concept of reason. Most of all, though, the Underground Man appeals against the enthronement of economic well-being as the measure of human action, famously saying that the idea of profit ignores the "maximally profitable profit" — free will. Noting that the second part of *Notes from Underground*, "Apropos of the Wet Snow," is set in the mid-1840s, around the time of Dostoevsky's literary debut with the sentimental epistolary novel *Poor Folk*, Joseph Frank has suggested that "the novella is above all a diptych depicting two episodes of a symbolic history of the Russian intelligentsia."[4] Breaking with the radicals of the 1860s, Dostoevsky was also signaling a break with his own past and declaring spiritual values above and beyond any practical measure.

No less important was Dostoevsky's rejection of Chernyshevsky's utilitarian aesthetics. In the introduction to *What Is to Be Done?* Chernyshevsky confessed, "I lack even a shade of artistic talent. I don't even have a good grasp of the language. But that's not important: read on, o kind public! Your reading of this book will not be devoid of utility. Truth is a good thing; it compensates for the failings of the writer who serves it."[5] Dostoevsky could not separate truth from form in this manner, and never could he view a narrative as a vessel of ideas, obliquely stated. On the contrary, the ideological debates of the 1860s formed no more than material in which Dostoevsky was minting an image of much greater lasting power. Chernyshevsky characterized his task as

4. Joseph Frank, *Dostoevsky: The Stir of Liberation, 1860-1865* (Princeton: Princeton University Press, 1986), p. 316.

5. Nikolai Chernyshevskii, *Chto delat'? Iz rasskazov o novykh liudiakh* (Leningrad, 1975), p. 14. The best edition in English is Nikolai Chernyshevsky, *What Is to Be Done?*, translated by Michael R. Katz, annotated by William G. Wagner (Ithaca and London: Cornell University Press, 1989); these passages occur on pp. 48-49.

the formation of a new public: "If you were the public," Chernyshevsky explained to his knowing readers, "I would no longer need to write. If you didn't exist, I couldn't write. But though you are not yet the public, you already exist among the public, so I must still and can already write." Chernyshevsky addressed his work to a new collective, one that eventually would take power in Russia, and one on which he depended to justify his work. Dostoevsky, by contrast, used the public sphere to speak directly to individuals in a work that was its own provocation and justification. Relinquishing the comfort of conventional form and medium, Dostoevsky placed a wager on the power of literature to enable moral and spiritual agency.

The Form of the Underground

Dostoevsky wrote *Notes from Underground* over a period of several months, from the end of 1863 to early 1864. This was a tumultuous time in Dostoevsky's life. His wife, Maria Dmitrievna, lay dying of tuberculosis. Moreover, *Vremia* had suddenly been banned in May 1863 because of an article in the April 1863 issue concerning the Polish uprising, and the brothers Dostoevsky were frantically trying to get out its successor, called *Epokha (Epoch)*. Dostoevsky felt that *Notes from Underground* (originally consisting of three parts) should be published all at once, but he rushed to get the first part ("The Underground") into the inaugural issue of *Epokha* (March-April 1864) and was forced to leave the rest for later. An editorial note signed by Mikhail Dostoevsky reads, "The continuation of F. M. Dostoevsky's tale *Notes from Underground* has been postponed until the next issue because of the author's illness" (28-2: 405). The continuation was not ready for May, however, and part two (originally entitled "A Tale Apropos of the Wet Snow") was published only in the June issue of 1864.

The delay was exacerbated by the censor's intervention in the first part of the *Notes* (especially, it would seem, what is now its tenth section). After perusing the journal, Dostoevsky wrote, furious, to his brother:

The misprints are terrible and it would have been better not to print the penultimate chapter at all (the main one, where the very idea is enunciated) than to print it as it is, with forced phrases and contradicting itself. What can you do! The censors are pigs; wherever I ridiculed everything and at times blasphemed *for show* — that was let by, but where I derived from this the need for faith and Christ — this was prohibited. Are they, the censors, in a plot against the government or something? (28-2: 73)

Since the manuscript has not survived, we can only guess what exactly the censor excised and how accurately Dostoevsky characterized its significance; he was not immune to exaggeration. Be that as it may, he began the second part, "Apropos of the Wet Snow," with the knowledge that the positive elements of the Underground Man's rant had been lost, and one can thus surmise that the narrative was written in part to compensate for the excisions and provide the lacking "need for faith and Christ." Dostoevsky's inability to spell things out explicitly forced him to wager on the reader's ability to construct a finished image out of disparate elements. To a large degree, any critical reading of *Notes from Underground* rests on how one reconciles the two parts of the work.

The story of the work shows that it would be wrong to view it merely as a defense of free will and a rejoinder to Chernyshevsky. This was a frequent mistake in the twentieth century, made by existentialists and cold warriors alike, who sometimes published the first part of *Notes from Underground* without the longer second part as a bold defense of free will. The editor's note accompanying the first publication contained an additional sentence that urged readers to regard the "first fragment" as "an introduction to the entire book, almost a preface" (5: 342). In letters to his brother, Dostoevsky expressly argued against publishing the parts of the work separately from each other, fearing that this would upset the intricate linkages between them, which he likened to "transitions" in music: "The first chapter appears to be chatter, but suddenly in the last two chapters this chatter is resolved in an unexpected catastrophe," he wrote to Mikhail on 13 April 1864. Further light is shed on the nature of this catastrophic resolution by another of Dostoevsky's intriguing comments to his brother concerning his work on the "tale": "In tone it is too strange, and the tone is shrill and wild; some people might not like it. Therefore it is necessary that poetry soften and salvage [*vynesla*] everything" (28-2: 70). We are left, then, with the question of where to seek the "poetry" of part two and how it proves "the need for faith and Christ." One answer lies in another episode of Dostoevsky's tumultuous biography.

The Wager and the Wet Snow

At the beginning of August 1863 — after publishing *Winter Notes on Summer Impressions* in February and March, and before beginning *Notes from Underground* — Dostoevsky set off on another long trip to Western Europe, where he met up with his lover, the twenty-three-year-old Apollinaria Suslova. Though he claimed the trip was intended to treat his epilepsy, which had first afflicted him in prison in 1850, Dostoevsky also spent a lot of time in casinos, frittering away sorely needed money, much of it borrowed. Left behind in Petersburg were Dostoevsky's terminally ill wife and his wayward stepson, Pavel Isaev, both of whom could have used his support. Also in need of his support was his brother, who was reeling from the prohibition of *Vremia* at the end of May. Dostoevsky kept an eye on all this as best he could, but the stress undermined any benefit he derived for his health.

Dostoevsky's actions represent a continual assertion of freedom against the combined forces of necessity, whether financial, social, or moral. Whether or not his epilepsy heightened his sensitivity to financial and erotic risk-taking, he always seemed ready and even eager to lodge a wager on the freedom of the future against the constraints of the present. Not that this faith in providence was ever borne out materially. As Joseph Frank has pointed out, through his gambling Dostoevsky "was paradoxically affirming his acceptance of the proper order of the universe as he conceived of it, and learning the same lesson as the underground man and all of his great negative heroes beginning with Raskolnikov, who deludedly believe they can master and suppress the irrational promptings of Christian conscience."[6] Dostoevsky's experiences in the summer of 1863 eventually resulted in his novella *The Gambler* (1866), but before that, they shaped the personality of the Underground Man, whose loss of faith in higher realities causes him constantly to hedge petty wagers with ever-diminishing returns. The issue was not to suppress the passion for wagers by limiting desire even more stringently to the bounds of scientific or dogmatic reason, but rather to redeem desire by raising the stakes of its wagers to the absolute limit, beyond what is commonly held to be rational or even possible.

But how can the Underground Man's petty hedges yield these absolute winnings? The diatribe in the first part of the novella has tended to overpower the hesitant resolution provided in the sequel. In one of the very few contemporary responses, the radical writer Mikhail Saltykov-Shchedrin provided a parody of the *Notes:* "The stage is neither dark nor light, but of some greyish hue; living voices are not audible, only a hissing, and living images are not visible, but it is as if bats are crossing through the twilight air. It is not a fantastic world but not a living one either, rather it is as if made of jelly" (5: 382). Responding to rumors about Dostoevsky's "scandalous story," even Apollinaria Suslova expressed concern that Dostoevsky was becoming "cynical" (5: 379). It must have pained him to hear this — one of very few responses to the work that reached him — since he had put so much effort into the narrative refutation of the Underground Man's rant.

But then, the refutation of the Underground Man by the prostitute Liza is not an argument at all; she is not empowered to speak for herself in the work. Rather, the refutation emerges from her silence. Like some of Dostoevsky's later heroines, most notably the titular character of "The Gentle Creature" (1876), Liza remains a mute image hung over the narrative, testifying to the possibility of redemption beyond speech. The crucial move here is that, though the Underground Man might presently be in a prison of his own construction, the investigation of his

6. Frank, *Dostoevsky: The Stir of Liberation, 1860-1865,* p. 263.

past reveals moments of lost potentiality, most notably when Liza extends her love. The work moves from the cold, hard facts of social condition to the possibility of spiritual causation. Liza's love is a pledge that he might still be able to redeem, though this would require a wager that he finds impossible: a wager on the other.

Like so many of the experiences he related in his fiction, this was something Dostoevsky knew from personal experience. As he finished *Notes from Underground,* he was close to despair. His beloved brother died on 10 July 1864, endangering *Epokha* and leaving Dostoevsky saddled with debts for the rest of his life. A few months earlier, on 16 April 1864, he witnessed the death of his wife. He wrote to a friend that she "had loved me boundlessly, and I loved her also without measure, but we did not live happily together" (28-2: 116). Her death led Dostoevsky to record some of his loftiest words about human potential:

> Maria is lying on the table. Will I ever see Maria?
>
> To love another man *as oneself,* according to Christ's testament, is impossible. The law of the personality binds us on earth. The *I* gets in the way. Only Christ could, but Christ was the ideal eternal from the ages, to which man strives and should strive, according to the law of nature. At the same time, after the appearance of Christ as *an ideal of man in the flesh* it has become as clear as day that the highest, final development of the person is precisely [. . .] so that man found, realized, and believed with all the power of his nature that the highest use he can make of his person . . . is, as it were, to destroy this *I* and give it to all and to any without separation and without regret. [. . .] So, on earth man strives for an ideal *opposite* to his nature. Whenever man has failed to fulfill the law of striving for the ideal, that is, when he has not sacrificed in love his *I* to people or another being (Maria and I), he feels suffering and has named this state "sin." Thus, man should incessantly feel suffering, which is balanced by the heavenly pleasure of fulfilling the law, that is, by sacrifice. This is earthly balance. Otherwise the earth would be meaningless. (20: 172-75)

In the face of such personal trauma, one might expect Dostoevsky to have behaved with more caution, but *Notes from Underground* shows how, out of the depths of dire necessity, he bet on a response of love.

The Ethics of Media

Dostoevsky's immersion in the mainstream media of his day was somewhat ironic, given the price he had paid for his previous involvement in illicit networks of textual production, dissemination, and performance. His arrest on 23 April 1849 had been instigated by his reading of correspondence between Nikolai Gogol and Vissarion Belinsky, in which the young critic had excoriated the older writer for his declarations of fidelity to the Orthodox Church, which Belinsky associated with the repressive autocracy. In the course of long interrogations, Dostoevsky insisted that he read the incriminating letters out of pure interest, having been an acolyte of Gogol and a protégé of Belinsky, and that "he did not agree with a single one of the exaggerations found in this article" (18: 180). However during their search of Dostoevsky's flat, the police also confiscated two banned books, a socialist tract by Eugène Sue and a critique of religion by P. J. Proudhon, thereby confirming their suspicion that Dostoevsky was trafficking in sedition. It was for these crimes that on 22 December 1849 Dostoevsky received a death sentence that at the last minute was commuted by the emperor to four years in prison and six more in exile as a soldier. It was a good thing for Dostoevsky that the authorities never learned of his involvement in a more serious plot to establish an illicit printing press.

In the fictional works he wrote after returning to St. Petersburg, Dostoevsky constantly highlighted the various networks of textual transmission and circulation. Prior to committing murder, Raskolnikov calls attention to himself by publishing a newspaper article.[7] The world

7. On the media sources of Dostoevsky's novels, see Konstantine Klioutchkine, "The Rise of *Crime and Punishment* from the Air of the Media," *Slavic Review* 61, no. 1 (Spring 2002): 88-108; and Anne Lounsbery, "Print Culture and Real Life in Dostoevskii's *Demons*," *Dostoevsky Studies*, n.s., 11 (2007): 25-37.

of *Demons* is awash in illicit and inflammatory texts, both smuggled into Russia from abroad and printed domestically on underground presses, including Stavrogin's scandalous confession. Ivan Karamazov is the author of published and unpublished theological texts. As these examples show, within the dense media sphere of Dostoevsky's novels, the official press tends to produce more noise than understanding.

Upon close analysis, one notes that the Underground Man is constantly speaking in words borrowed from the contemporary media. The ideals against which he measures himself, and against which he then rebels, are imposed from without. He imagines how various scenarios will play out, only to realize that they are derivative of popular literary works. Only in his memory of Liza can he hear someone speaking to him as an individual, and only in response to her can he imagine himself saying something sincere, though his over-reflective consciousness prevents him from actually doing so. Only in such a private encounter could he reconcile himself to an open future, as opposed to the neat images of success that confront him at every turn in the public sphere. However, in the totalizing media world, even this private encounter is tainted by the Underground Man's consciousness of its possible literary models and by his constant sense of shame, as if he is perpetually being scrutinized by an audience; therefore, he feigns haughty indifference and self-reliance. His final gesture shows him decisively choosing his projected, finalized identity over the more difficult restoral of emotional immediacy. As Gary Saul Morson has remarked, "Closure and structure mark the difference between life as it is lived and as it is read about; and real people live without the benefit of an outside perspective on which both closure and structure depend."[8] The wall against which the Underground Man flails consists of words and images which can never be his own.

Notes from Underground powerfully affirms the unrealized potentialities within media culture and its ability to allow unsightly reality to form itself into an image. In Part One we see the Underground Man rail-

8. Gary Saul Morson, *Narrative and Freedom: The Shadows of Time* (New Haven and London: Yale University Press, 1994), p. 38.

ing against a conventional wisdom derived from newspapers and journals, but instead of simply explaining his current state, the narrative of Part Two also reveals points at which another kind of connection was possible between the Underground Man and others, especially Liza. Freedom from the necessity of the present may lie in the future, but only through the mediation of the past. The Underground Man's autobiographical notes reveal a potential for being loved, and therefore, perhaps, for loving another, though his inability to bring the story to a close prevents the notes from reaching any listeners who might hear him. The editor's decision to end the text at Liza's departure, though the story goes on incessantly, marks a point where the text recedes before the enormity of a life, which can only be suggested, never captured, on the page.

Dostoevsky's Notes

Dostoevsky's works of the early 1860s represent his first attempts not only to escape the logic of the modern media but also to create a Christian literature. As Dostoevsky's works make abundantly clear, this did not necessarily mean a literature about Christianity or even about Christians. Working out what it did mean brought Dostoevsky face-to-face with a fundamental question: How can art communicate ideas through form? His answer was that Christianity revealed nothing other than a new concept of image, and that therefore art is Christian above all not in its ideas, but in the kind of image it projects.

Dostoevsky's view of the sovereign power of art had deep roots in his earlier career. In the course of his interrogations when he was under arrest in 1849, Dostoevsky presented an impassioned defense of the need for writers to enjoy freedom in their art. "Society cannot exist without literature," he said, insofar as literature serves as "the mirror of society" (18: 126). He insisted that he did not mean the freedom to utter seditious ideas, but rather the purely artistic freedom to choose subject and style; this was the freedom of imagination, not the freedom of speech. His standpoint here brought him into conflict both with the censors (who suspected criminal intent in any satire or tragedy) and with radical critics like Belinsky, whom Dostoevsky described as "[trying] to give literature a limited and undignified role, reducing it to the mere description, so to speak, of *purely newspaper facts* and scandalous events" (18: 127). In short, Dostoevsky remarked, "literature needs no tendency; art is a goal in itself; the artist should simply concern himself with artistry and the idea will come of its own accord, for it is a necessary condition of artistry" (18: 128-29).

One influential view has focused on Dostoevsky's use of the term *image (obraz)* as a counterpoint to the *unsightliness (bezobrazie)* he observed in modern life.[9] But how would Dostoevsky's image differ from a purely imaginary and therefore innocuous construct like the utopia of Vera Pavlovna's fourth dream in Chernyshevsky's *What Is to Be Done?* After his arrest in 1849 as part of a group linked to Mikhail Petrashevsky, a follower of French utopian Charles Fourier, Dostoevsky remarked, "As far as we — Russia, Petersburg — are concerned, it's enough to walk twenty paces along the street to become convinced that on our soil Fourierism can exist only in the uncut pages of a book or in a soft, gentle, and dreamy soul, but in no other form than that of an idyll or a verse poem in twenty-four cantos" (18: 133). Such images eviscerate the reality they describe; they characterize the media which comprise the Underground Man's world and which prove helpless against his destructive cynicism. It is difficult to identify any hardier image that might counteract the unsightliness of the Underground Man. Even Liza is disfigured by her sordid surroundings.

Clarification can be had if we take a closer look at the genre of *Notes from Underground.* Along with *Notes from the Dead House* and *Winter Notes on Summer Impressions,* it is one of three works by Dostoevsky from this period that exhibit the tension between eternal questions and topical crises. The three works are united by the use of a first-person narrator who struggles to make sense of the chaotic life that surrounds him without eviscerating it. A defining feature of these "notes" is their

9. See Jackson, *The Art of Dostoevsky;* see also Jackson, *Dostoevsky's Quest for Form: A Study of His Philosophy of Art,* 2d ed. (Bloomington, Ind.: Physsardt Publishers, 1978).

narrator's mimicry of dominant ideological standpoints. (Dostoevsky himself was an accomplished impersonator and enthusiastic participant in amateur theatricals.) To a large degree, these three sets of "notes" are more of a visceral record of social disfiguration than an attempt to impose or even reveal an image.

Dostoevsky's genre of "notes" is analogous to his account of genre painting in an 1873 essay titled "At the Exhibition," which was published in his *Diary of a Writer.* Here he reiterates his long-standing rejection of tendentiousness in art, lamenting that because of the call for social relevance, "a young poet resists his natural need to pour forth in his own images [. . .] and forces himself painfully to produce a topic that satisfies the general, uniform, liberal and social opinion" (21: 73). Addressing the tradition typified by the radical critics Nikolai Chernyshevsky and Nikolai Dobroliubov, Dostoevsky continues, " 'One must represent reality as it is,' they say; meanwhile, there is no such reality and there never has been on earth, because the essence of things is inaccessible to man, and he perceives nature as it is reflected in his idea and filtered through his feelings" (21: 75). Dostoevsky begins by distinguishing the problem of representation in various artistic genres, each of which treats the relationship between image and idea differently. The portraitist, for instance, must capture the moment when the subject is most like himself. The historical painter, by contrast, must capture the original moment and its future potentiality, which explains why this moment has deserved commemoration. But how does the genre painter capture the idea and the as-yet-unrealized potential of the present moment? This is precisely Dostoevsky's problem in *Notes:* to provide a visceral image of a reality that is disfigured, unsightly, and inchoate. This is especially true of the first part; as a historical narrative, the second part also manifests alternative potentialities, but to be realized, these potentialities would require someone — the Underground Man, his editor, or (most likely) his readers — to take the absolute risk of faith.

In his "editor's note" to *Notes from Underground,* Dostoevsky claims that the Underground Man is a necessary fiction. "Such persons as the writer of these notes not only may, but even must, exist in our society," he writes, but only as "one of the representatives of a generation now coming to an end." The Underground Man represents an unproductive present that bears within itself all the inevitability of the past. An analogous formulation appears in the note "From the Author" to *The Brothers Karamazov,* where Dostoevsky calls Alyosha an "odd man" who nonetheless "carries within himself the heart of the whole" (14: 5). Alyosha represents a present that is open to the future and bears within it all the unrealized potentialities of the past. These two prefaces describe the progress of Dostoevsky's imagination during the last twenty years of his life, from the Underground Man to the new saint, from the tyrannous present to the as-yet-free future, and from the compulsive author to the responsive reader. This hard-fought progress was Dostoevsky's ultimate wager.

Suggestions for Further Reading

Mikhail Bakhtin. *Problems of Dostoevsky's Poetics.* Translated and edited by Caryl Emerson. Minneapolis: University of Minnesota Press, 1984. This is a fascinating and influential study of Dostoevsky's fiction as an innovative form of ideological discourse.

Nikolai Chernyshevsky. *What Is to Be Done?* Translated by Michael R. Katz; annotated by William G. Wagner. Ithaca and London: Cornell University Press, 1989.

Fyodor Dostoevsky. *Notes from Underground.* 2d edition. Translated and edited by Michael Katz. New York and London: W. W. Norton, 2001. This Norton Critical Edition includes enlightening background sources and critical responses.

Fyodor Dostoevsky. *Winter Notes on Summer Impressions.* Translated by David Patterson. Evanston, Ill.: Northwestern University Press, 1988.

Joseph Frank. *Dostoevsky: The Stir of Liberation, 1860-1865.* Princeton: Princeton University Press, 1986. This volume is the third part of Frank's magisterial biography of the writer.

René Girard. *Resurrection from the Underground: Feodor Dostoevsky.* Edited and translated by James G. Williams. New York: Crossroad,

1997. Girard takes the "underground" as a starting point for a wide-ranging reflection on Dostoevsky's work.

Robert Louis Jackson. *The Art of Dostoevsky: Deliriums and Nocturnes.* Princeton: Princeton University Press, 1981. Jackson's close readings of individual works, including *Notes from Underground,* are unparalleled in their sensitivity and insight.

Gary Saul Morson. *Narrative and Freedom: The Shadows of Time.* New Haven: Yale University Press, 1994. This is a philosophical meditation on narrative that features, *inter alia,* analyses of *Notes from Underground.*

James P. Scanlan. *Dostoevsky the Thinker.* Ithaca and London: Cornell University Press, 2002. Scanlan's volume offers the most complete and authoritative account of Dostoevsky's interest in and relevance for specific philosophical problems.

Translator's Preface

Let me caution the reader: This translation uses coarser language than any previous one. In fact, I use a well-known four-letter word[1] which I hope does not offend readers. I think that if the Underground Man were writing today, many of his "viles" and "fouls" would be replaced by words far nastier than any I know. Some of our contemporary American writers (e.g., Bellow, Roth, and especially Pynchon) do not shy away from such words, and the Underground Man is certainly as rude as any of them. When it was first published (in 1864), the book was — philosophically and even terminologically — shocking, and my use of a four-letter word is an effort to regain some of the book's original shock value, thus producing a fresh translation for our ruder times.

But, of course, there is much more to Dostoevsky's book (and, hopefully, my translation) than rudeness and the desire to shock. Ideally, the translator is the author's most careful reader, penetrating more deeply than any other reader into the interstices of the text. As such a "deep reader," I have observed that the Underground Man's mind moves in circles, returning to certain clusters of terms and con-

---

1. This is not an arbitrary invention of mine. Dostoevsky uses the word *nagadit'* ("to do something vile to") in the first paragraph of the work. In popular speech, this word has the connotation of excrement, and I have translated it by using a certain four-letter word. Somehow, the overly polite scrutiny of the censors failed to notice this meaning. One should keep in mind that many of the "nasty" words used by the Underground Man — *gadkii* ("vile, nasty"), *gadost'* ("vileness, nastiness") — have the same root as *nagadit'*.

cepts; and I have realized that the translator's mind too must move in the same circles in order to capture all the nuances of these terms and concepts. What have I discovered through this deep reading? Let me note a few examples.

First of all, the Underground Man is obsessed with the idea of "vocation," probably because he doesn't have one and doesn't want one, except to be a lazy idler. With regard to vocation, this is what he says about himself:

> I'm living out my life in my corner, taunting myself with the angry and useless consolation that an intelligent man cannot seriously become anything, but that only a fool can become something. . . . Question: Who are you? Answer: A lazy idler. . . . "Lazy idler!" That's a vocation and a mission; that's a career, gentlemen.

Thus, it follows that all people with settled professions — carpenters, writers, dictators, bishops, theologians, housewives, cooks, dancers, terrorists — are fools. I think the Underground Man would forgive people if they worked in order to eat or to support their families (or maybe he wouldn't), but he would certainly despise and mock people who wanted to make something of themselves. You might ask him, "Isn't it natural to want to make something of yourself? At the very least, that would expand the opportunities of one's life, enrich it, increase one's enjoyments." But he might answer, "Yes, enrich what's worthless with more worthless trash; increase the enjoyment of what is vain and vulgar."

So, the best thing is to be a lazy idler. You wouldn't have any commerce with your fellow men, and you could stay apart from the insults and frustrations of everyday life. But, you might ask, wouldn't the world end if everyone became an idler? "So what?" the Underground Man would probably answer. "Let it end!" Though, of course, it won't end: the frustrations and insults will keep coming until the sun finally explodes and swallows our earth.

Then, there is the Underground Man's attitude toward consciousness:

I swear to you, gentlemen, that to be overly conscious — is a disease, a real and full-fledged disease. For common human purposes, it would be more than sufficient to possess ordinary human consciousness, that is, even fifty percent or twenty-five percent less than the amount of consciousness available to the cultivated man of our unhappy nineteenth century. . . .

So, it would appear that unconsciousness (or at least a very low degree of consciousness) is better. Although something tells me that the Underground Man is one of those poor saps with an overly acute consciousness. Or maybe one of those poor mice:

And the main thing, after all, is that he himself [i.e., the man of overly acute consciousness] . . . regards himself as a mouse; no one asks him to do so; and that's an important point.

And so, the more acute your consciousness, the more you approach the animal kingdom. Interesting. Perhaps the febrile consciousness is more animal than human, and man is more animal spirit than consciousness. And what is the significance of all the animals in the *Notes* — the mice and the ants? Nabokov liked to call the story "Memoirs from a Mousehole" (*podpolie* literally means "under the floor," the home of mice and other vermin).[2]
And then there is the famous "wall":

Impossibility — in other words, a stone wall! . . . There's something calming, morally resolving, and final in the wall, perhaps even something mystical. . . . It goes without saying that I won't break through such a wall with my forehead if I actually don't have the strength to break through it, but I won't make peace

2. The work has not always been called in English "Notes from Underground." A very early translation calls it "Memoirs from the Underworld." ("Underworld," of course, implies something entirely different in American English.) Sometimes, the work has been called "Notes from *the* Underground." It would be interesting to explore the implications of this "the."

with it either just because I have a stone wall here but lack the strength.

The Underground Man has probably spent more time staring at walls (in his apartment) than any hundred inhabitants of Petersburg combined. Maybe his dream (he's constantly dreaming) is to pierce through these walls and to enter into the cosmic (or heavenly?) spaces — into some trans-mural domain. He does venture into billiard rooms and houses of prostitution, but that's not the same thing. And he also goes into the streets of Petersburg, but if you've ever been there, you know that this gray, icy, underground-like city is the least trans-mural place in the world: eternally black-and-white sky; huge, monumental, disconcerting buildings enclosing you on all sides; and a swamp beneath you. Wandering around this city, your only desire is to find yourself warm and cozy between four walls.

By the way, speaking of the Underground Man's environment, the Russian émigré critic Georgy Meier has pointed out (in *The Light Shining in the Night*, his groundbreaking study of *Crime and Punishment*) that Dostoevsky's characters tend to project their internal world into the outside world; for example, their apartments become a mirror image of their souls (e.g., Raskolnikov and his "kennel" of a room). Thus, the Underground (and perhaps the whole underground city, Petersburg) is a projection, a reflection, an outward manifestation, an emanation, a carbon-copy image of the Underground Man's soul. It may be that the wall itself is something that emanates from him.

Then there is the mathematical or quantitative side of *Notes from Underground*. Has anyone noticed that the Underground Man uses a lot of locutions and analogies rooted in the world of mathematics and engineering? (Remember that Dostoevsky got a degree in engineering.) He constantly keeps talking about mathematical tables and statistics, about test tubes and chemical reactions. He's constantly telling us how long things take (e.g., two minutes) and the distance people have traveled (e.g., two hundred paces). And then there's the famous "two times two equals four":

But, all the same, two times two equals four is an awfully insufferable thing. Two times two equals four — why, in my opinion, it's nothing but insolence, gentlemen. Two times two equals four is a cocky dude who stands with his hands on his hips blocking your way and spitting at you. I agree that two times two equals four is a superb thing, but if we're to give everything its due, two times two equals five is sometimes a very splendid little thing too.

He's telling us that mathematicized, technological civilization has certain defects. But in the twenty-first century, we know that better than he does: the atom bomb is the product, par excellence, of $2 \times 2 = 4$ (or is it a product of $2 \times 2 = 5$?).

And then there's the Underground Man's famous reference to "living life":[3]

Because I was unaccustomed to it, "living life" oppressed me to the point where I had trouble breathing.

But what is "living life"? Compare this to what D. H. Lawrence once wrote: "To be alive, to be man alive, to be whole man alive: that is the point. . . . So much of man walks about dead and a carcass in the street and house, today; so much of woman is merely dead. Like a pianoforte with half the notes mute."[4] So, "living life" must mean an intensity of life overflowing the bounds of ordinary life, a life (to use a mathematical term the Underground Man might have approved of) exponentially

3. Was the Underground Man familiar with the twelfth-century mystical theologians Bernard of Clairvaux (who speaks of *vivida vita et vitalis*), William of Saint-Thierry (who speaks of *vita vivens*), and Thomas de Froidmont (who speaks of *vita vitalis*), or with the Flemish mystic Ruysbroeck (who speaks of *levende leven*)?

4. It is an interesting coincidence that Lawrence writes about human degradation in terms of a piano with mute notes while the Underground Man speaks of it in terms of piano keys and organ stops. Interesting also to compare this to something Pascal said: "People think that you can play on a man as you play on an organ. An organ he is in truth, but a strange and fitful one. He who can play only on an ordinary organ will produce no chords from this one." Or Hamlet and the recorder.

greater than the life most human beings allow themselves to be capable of.[5]

Let me end this survey with one of my favorite paragraphs from the *Notes:*

> In the last analysis, gentlemen, it's better to do nothing! The best thing is conscious inertia! And so, long live the underground! Even though I said that I envy the normal man with all my bile, still I don't want to be him in the circumstances in which I see him (although, all the same, I won't stop envying him). No, no, the underground is, in any case, more profitable! There one can at least . . . Oh, but even now I'm lying! I'm lying because I myself know, like two times two, that it's not at all the underground that's better, but something different, totally different, for which I'm thirsting, but which I can't ever find! To hell with the underground![6]

What is this thing that's better? Is it God? Is it the Kingdom of Heaven? Can the Underground Man be lapsing into hope and faith? I don't believe it. Next thing you know, he'll be going to church. (No, he's too lazy for that — he'd never stand for three hours at a Russian Orthodox liturgy.) But the "Kingdom of Heaven" has a nice ring to it. Maybe even a nicer ring than the "Underground."

---

5. By the way, other translators of this work have chosen not to use the phrase "living life," thinking it redundant and using instead a paraphrase. But is it really redundant?

6. Note that this passage is replete with some of the Underground Man's favorite notions — idleness (here, inertia), consciousness, profit, and "two times two."

NOTES FROM UNDERGROUND

PART ONE

The Underground

I

I'm a sick man. . . . I'm an evil man. I'm an unattractive man. I think my liver is sick: it hurts. But I really don't understand squat about my sickness, and I'm not sure what hurts inside me. I'm not being treated, and have never been treated, even though I have respect for medicine and doctors. I'm also extremely superstitious — in fact, so superstitious that I even have respect for medicine. (I'm sufficiently educated not to be superstitious, but I *am* superstitious.) No, gentlemen, it's because I'm evil that I don't want to receive treatment. You, on your part, probably can't understand this. Well, sir, *I* understand it. Of course, I wouldn't be able to explain to you who exactly I'm trying to annoy by being evil; I know perfectly well that the doctors don't give a shit if I'm refusing their

---

Dostoevsky's note: The author of these "Notes" and the "Notes" themselves are, of course, fictitious. Nevertheless, such persons as the writer of these notes not only may, but even must, exist in our society, when we take into account the circumstances in the case of which our society has been formed. I have tried to expose one of the characters of the recent past to the view of the public more distinctly than is commonly done. He is one of the representatives of a generation now coming to an end. In this fragment, entitled "The Underground," this person introduces himself and his views, and, as it were, tries to clarify the reasons why he has made his appearance and was bound to make his appearance in our midst. The subsequent fragment will contain the actual "Notes" of this person concerning certain events in his life.

treatment; I know better than anyone that all this is hurting only me, nobody else. Nevertheless, if I'm not seeking treatment, it's because I'm evil and angry. My liver is sick and it hurts — well, let it hurt even more!

I've been living this way for a long time — for about twenty years. I'm forty years old now. I used to work in the civil service, but I no longer do. I was an evil and angry official. I was rude, and found pleasure in rudeness. After all, since I didn't take bribes, I had to reward myself in some other way. (A lame joke; but I won't cross it out. When I wrote it, I thought it would be very witty; but now when I see that I wrote it because I wanted to engage in a kind of vile swagger — I won't cross it out on purpose!) When petitioners would approach my desk for information, I'd gnash my teeth at them, and feel an insatiable pleasure if I succeeded in disappointing someone. And I almost always succeeded. For the most part these were timid people — petitioners, after all. But among the dandies there was a certain officer I particularly couldn't stand. He absolutely didn't want to submit to me, but instead would bang his saber in the most repulsive way. For a year and a half, he and I fought a war over this saber. And I finally prevailed. He stopped banging it. However, all this happened when I was still young. But do you know, gentlemen, what constituted the crux of my anger? The whole point of it, the really vile thing was that, every moment, even at those moments when I could taste the bitterest bile rising up in me, I was shamefully conscious that not only was I not angry on this occasion, but that I'm not even a fundamentally angry man, that I was only uselessly scaring sparrows and finding consolation in that. I could be foaming at the mouth, but if you were to bring me some little doll, or some tea with sugar, I might calm down and my heart might even be touched, although later I would probably gnash my teeth at myself and, out of shame, suffer from sleeplessness for a few months. Such is my custom.

I lied about myself just now when I said I was an evil and angry official. I lied out of anger. I was just playing with the petitioners and with the officer; I could never really become evil and angry. At every moment I was conscious that I contained in myself a multitudinous multitude of elements totally opposite to that. I felt them swarming inside me, these opposite elements. I knew that they'd been swarming inside me my entire life, and asking to be let out; but I wasn't letting them out, wasn't letting them out on purpose. They were torturing me to the point of shame; they were driving me to convulsions; and finally I got fed up with them — how fed up I got with them! Doesn't it even seem to you, gentlemen, that I'm repenting of something before you now, that I'm asking your forgiveness for something? I'm certain that's how it seems to you. . . . But, I assure you, I don't care if that's how it seems. . . .

Not only couldn't I become evil; I couldn't become anything — either evil or good, either a villain or an honorable man, either a hero or an insect. And now I'm living out my days in my corner, taunting myself with the angry and useless consolation that an intelligent man cannot seriously become anything, but that only a fool becomes something. Yes, gentlemen, an intelligent man of the nineteenth century must be, and is morally obliged to be, fundamentally a being without character; whereas a man with character, a man of action, must be, and is morally obliged to be, a fundamentally limited being. That's my conviction at the age of forty. I'm forty years old, and forty years — that's an entire lifetime. It's extreme old age. To live beyond forty is indecent, vulgar, and immoral! Answer me, sincerely and honestly: who lives beyond forty? I'll tell you: fools and villains. Let all the elders come up to me, all those venerable elders, all those silver-haired and fragrant elders; and I'll say this right to their face! Let the whole world come up to me, and I'll say it right to its face! I have the right to talk this way, because I myself am going to live to the age of sixty. I'm going to live to seventy! I'm going to live to eighty! . . . Wait! I need to catch my breath. . . .

You're probably thinking, gentlemen, that I want to amuse you? Here, too, you're wrong. I'm really not such a merry fellow as it seems to you, or as it may seem to you; however, if you're irritated by all this blather (and I feel that you're already irritated) and think of asking me, Who exactly am I? — I'll answer you: I'm just a collegiate assessor.[1] I served in the civil service so that I could eat (and only for that reason);

---

1. This rank was the eighth of the fourteen ranks in the Table of Ranks of the Imperial Russian civil service. To reach this rank is an unimpressive achievement. *Trans.*

and when last year one of my distant relatives left me six thousand roubles in his will, I retired at once and took up residence here in my corner. Even before this, I had lived in this corner; but now I've taken up residence in this corner. My room is squalid and vile — it's on the edge of the city. My servant is an old peasant woman, spiteful out of stupidity; and she always smells bad. I've been told that the Petersburg climate is doing me harm and that with my limited resources, it's very expensive for me to live in Petersburg. I know all this; I know it better than all these experienced and ultra-wise busybodies who like to give advice. But I'm going to remain in Petersburg; I'm not leaving Petersburg! I'm not leaving because . . . Oh, what difference does it make whether I leave or stay?

By the way: What can a respectable man talk about with the greatest pleasure?

Answer: about himself.

So then I, too, will talk about myself.

II

I now want to tell you, gentlemen, whether you desire to hear it or do not desire to hear it, why I never succeeded in becoming even an insect. Let me tell you solemnly that, many times, I desired to become an insect. But I wasn't worthy even of that. I swear to you, gentlemen, that to be acutely conscious is a sickness, a real and full-fledged sickness. For common human purposes, it would be more than sufficient to possess ordinary human consciousness — that is, even 50 percent or 25 percent less than the amount of consciousness available to the cultivated man of our unhappy nineteenth century, and especially to a cultivated man who is unfortunate enough to live in Petersburg, the most abstract and premeditated city on the face of the earth. (There are premeditated cities and unpremeditated cities.) It would be more than sufficient, for example, to possess the kind of consciousness by which all the so-called spontaneous people and men of action live. I bet you think I'm writing all this out of a kind of conceited swagger, in order to crack jokes at the expense of the men of action, and that because of this tasteless swagger, I'm even banging a saber, like my officer. But, gentlemen, who takes pride in his sicknesses and even shows them off with a conceited swagger?

But what am I saying? All people do it: they all take pride in their sicknesses; and I do it perhaps more than anyone else. Let's not argue; my objection is absurd. Nevertheless, here's what I'm absolutely certain of: not only too much consciousness, but even any consciousness at all is a sickness. I insist on this. But let's return to this a little later. Instead, tell me this: How did it happen that, as if on purpose, during those very same moments, yes, those very same moments when I was most capable of being conscious of all the subtleties of everything that was "beautiful and sublime," as they used to say here once upon a time[2] — how did it happen, then, that my consciousness would stop working and instead I would do such indecent things, things which . . . well, things, in short, which, even though everybody does them, perhaps, but which, as if on purpose, I did exactly when I was most conscious that they shouldn't be done at all? The more I was conscious of the good, and of all this "beautiful and sublime" stuff, the deeper I sank into my shit, and the more capable I was of becoming totally enmired in it. But here's the main thing: it was as if none of this was accidental in me; it was as if it all necessarily had to be. It was as if this was my natural condition, not some sickness and not some rot in me, so that, finally, I had lost all inclination to struggle against this rot. It ended by my almost believing (and maybe I really did believe) that this is perhaps in fact my normal condition. But first, in the beginning, you should have seen what agonies I endured in this struggle! I didn't believe that this happened to others too; and therefore all of my life I kept it hidden inside me, like a secret. I was ashamed (perhaps I'm ashamed even now); I reached the point where I would experience a kind of secret, abnormal, foul little pleasure in returning home to my corner on some vile Peters-

2. This phrase originated in Edmund Burke's *Philosophical Inquiry into the Origin of Our Ideas of the Sublime and Beautiful* (1756). This phrase became a commonplace in the writings of certain Russian critics of the 1840s, who saw in it the goal of all of man's strivings. Here, the Underground Man shows his contempt not only for this idea but for the entire spirit of the idealistic 1840s in Russia. *Trans.*

burg night, in being acutely conscious that, today too, I had done something foul and that it would be impossible to undo that which was done, and in inwardly, secretly gnawing, gnawing at myself with my teeth for this foul thing, biting and sucking at my own marrow until the bitterness finally turned into some sort of shameful, accursed sweetness and, finally, into definite and serious pleasure! Yes, into pleasure, into pleasure! I insist on this. I started talking about this because I want to know for certain whether other people have such pleasures. Let me explain it to you: the pleasure here resulted from an overly acute consciousness of one's humiliation; it resulted because you yourself now feel that you've reached the ultimate wall; because this may be vile, but it can't be any other way; because there's no way out for you now; because you'll never become another person; because even if there were still enough time and faith for you to change into something else, you probably wouldn't even want to change; and even if you wanted to, you wouldn't do anything even then, since, in reality, there's perhaps nothing for you to change into. But, mainly and in the final analysis, all this happens in accordance with the normal and fundamental laws of the overly acute consciousness and in accordance with the inertia directly following from these laws; and consequently, not only will you not change, but you simply won't do anything at all. For example, it follows as a consequence of the overly acute consciousness that a villain is right to be a villain, as if this can offer any consolation to a villain if he himself feels that he truly is a villain. But enough of this. . . . Damn, I've talked a blue streak, but what have I explained? How can one explain the pleasure here? But I *will* explain myself. . . . I will bring it all through to the end! Why else did I pick up my pen?

I, for example, am awfully vain and conceited. I'm mistrustful and easy to offend, like a hunchback or a dwarf; but to tell the truth there have been moments when, if somebody had slapped me in the face, I might even have been glad. I'm being serious: I would probably have been able to discover some sort of pleasure in being slapped, a pleasure of despair, of course; but the intensest pleasures can lurk in despair, especially when you're acutely conscious that there's no way out of your predicament. And here, in the case of the slap, you're conscious that you've been reduced to a piece of shit. But the main thing is that, however you slice it, it turns out that I'm always the first to be blamed for everything, and the most offensive thing is that I'm guilty without guilt, guilty according to the laws of nature, so to speak. And so, I'm guilty, first of all, because I'm more intelligent than everyone around me. (I've always regarded myself as more intelligent than everyone around me; and sometimes, believe it or not, I've even been ashamed of this. At least, all my life I've never been able to look directly into people's eyes, but have always looked sort of to the side.) I'm guilty, finally, because even if there were any magnanimity in me, I'd only be tormented more by the consciousness of its utter uselessness. After all, I probably wouldn't be able to do anything with my magnanimity: I wouldn't be able to forgive because the offender might have slapped me according to the laws of nature, and it's impossible to forgive the laws of nature; and I wouldn't be able to forget because, even though the laws of nature are responsible, it's offensive nonetheless. Finally, even if I wanted to be absolutely unmagnanimous — that is, even if I desired to revenge myself on the offender — I wouldn't be able to revenge myself on anyone for anything, because, most likely, I would never decide to do anything, even if I could. Why is it I would never decide to do anything? I'd like to say a couple of words about this in particular.

III

After all, people who know how to revenge themselves and in general to stand up for themselves — how, for example, do they do it? After all, they must become so possessed, let us suppose, by a feeling of vengeance that nothing remains in their being for this period of time except this feeling. Such a gentleman pushes his way straight to the goal like an enraged bull with lowered horns, and only a wall can stop him. (By the way: confronted with a wall, such gentlemen — that is, spontaneous people and men of action — genuinely give up. For them, a wall is not an evasion, as, for example, it is for us, people who think and, as a result, do nothing; it's not an excuse to turn back, an excuse which we ourselves usually don't believe, but which we are always very glad to have. No, they give up in all sincerity. For them, there's something calming, morally resolving, and final in the wall, maybe even something mystical. . . . But about the wall later.) Well, sirs, I consider such a man of action to be the real, normal man, just as tender Mother Nature herself wished to see him when she graciously gave birth to him on earth. I'm envious of such a man with all my bile. He's dumb — I won't argue with you about that. But how do you know — maybe a normal man should be dumb. Maybe that's even very beautiful. And what convinces me even more of the truth of this suspicion, so to speak, is that if you take, for example, the antithesis of the normal man — that is, the man of overly acute consciousness, who emerged, of course, not out of the womb of nature but out of a test tube (this is already almost mysticism, gentlemen, but that's my suspicion too) — this test-tube man sometimes gives up so completely in the face of his antithesis that he himself, with all his overly acute consciousness, genuinely regards himself not as a man but as a mouse. This may be an acutely conscious mouse, but it is a mouse nonetheless, whereas here we have a man, and consequently . . . etc., etc. And the main thing, after all, is that he himself, he himself regards himself as a mouse; no one asks him to do so; and that's an important point. Let us now view this mouse in action. Let us suppose, for example, that the mouse, too, is offended (and it is almost always offended), and that it, too, wants to revenge itself. It may be that this mouse contains even more accumulated anger than *l'homme de la nature et de la vérité*.[3] A vile, mean little desire to repay the offender with the same evil that it has received is, perhaps, festering in the mouse even more foully than in *l'homme de la nature et de la vérité*, because *l'homme de la nature et de la vérité*, with his congenital stupidity, considers his revenge to be nothing less than simple justice, whereas the mouse, as a consequence of its overly acute consciousness, denies there is any justice here. We get, finally, to the very deed, to the very act of revenge. The unfortunate mouse, in addi-

---

3. "The man of nature and of truth." This is a mocking reference to Jean-Jacques Rousseau, on whose tomb was inscribed: *Ici repose l'homme de la nature et de la vérité. Trans.*

tion to the one original vileness, has managed to amass around itself, in the form of questions and doubts, so many other vilenesses; to the one question it has added so many unresolved questions that, want it or not, around the mouse we get some sort of fatal slop, some sort of stinking filth, consisting of its doubts, worries, and finally of the spittle sprinkling down upon it from men of action who have solemnly assembled round as judges and dictators, and who are ridiculing it with their robust, full-throated laughter. Naturally, the only thing the mouse can do now is dismiss everything with a wave of its paw and, with a smile of simulated contempt, which it itself doesn't believe in, slip away shamefully into its hole. There, in its foul, stinking underground, our offended, beaten-down, ridiculed mouse immediately submerges itself in a cold, venomous, and — this is the main thing — eternal anger. For forty years without interruption it will remember its injury down to the last, most shameful details, and each time it will add even more shameful details of its own, spitefully taunting and irritating itself with its own fantasies. It will be ashamed of its fantasies, but nevertheless it will remember everything, pick through everything, think up things about itself that never happened under the pretext that they could have happened; and it will never forgive anything. It may even begin to revenge itself, but by fits and starts, in trivial things, from behind the stove, incognito, believing neither in its right to take revenge nor in the success of its revenge, and knowing in advance that from all its attempts at revenge it will suffer a hundred times more than the object of its vengeance, who might not even scratch himself. On its deathbed, it will again remember everything, with interest compounded over all those years and. . . . But this cold, disgusting semi-despair and semi-faith; this conscious self-burial alive in the underground for forty years from grief; this impasse which you have created for yourself with great effort but which is nevertheless somewhat dubious; this entire poison of unsatisfied desires, which have retreated inward; this fever of vacillations, of decisions made forever and of repentances which return after a minute — this is precisely the sap of that strange pleasure which I've been talking about. This pleasure is so subtle, so inaccessible sometimes to the consciousness, that even slightly limited people, or even just those who have strong nerves, won't understand a single thing about it. "Perhaps," you'll add, grinning broadly, "people who have never been slapped in the face won't understand it, either"; this is your polite way of hinting that I, too, in the course of my life, have perhaps been slapped in the face and that I am therefore speaking as an expert. I bet that's what you're thinking. But calm yourselves, gentlemen. I've never been slapped, although I'm totally indifferent to what you may think about this. I might even regret that, in the course of my life, I haven't slapped enough people. But enough: I won't say another word on this subject which you find so infinitely interesting.

Let me calmly continue what I was saying about people with strong nerves who don't understand certain subtle pleasures. In certain cases, for example, these gentlemen may bellow like bulls, from the bottom of their gullets, which may be to their greatest credit; but, as I've already said, they immediately become docile when confronted with impossibility. Impossibility — in other words, a stone wall! What stone wall? Well, naturally, the laws of nature, the conclusions of the natural sciences, mathematics. Once they've proved to you, for example, that you're descended from the ape, it's no use making faces — just accept it. And once they've proved to you that, in essence, one little drop of your own fat must be more precious to you than a hundred thousand of your fellow human beings, and that, as a result, this finally solves the problem of all so-called virtues and obligations and other such ravings and prejudices — you have to accept this too. Nothing can be done, because two times two is mathematics. Just try to object.

"Excuse me!" they'll yell at you. "Rebellion is impossible: this is two times two equals four! Nature doesn't consult with you; she doesn't care about your wishes or whether you like or dislike her laws. You're obliged to accept her as she is, and consequently all of her results. This means the wall is the wall . . . etc., etc." Good Lord, why should I care about the laws of nature and arithmetic if for some reason I dislike these laws and this "two times two equals four"? It goes without saying that I won't break through such a wall with my forehead if I actually don't have the strength to break through it, but I won't make peace with it either just because I have a stone wall here but lack the strength.[1]

As if such a stone wall could truly produce tranquility, could truly embody some word concerning peace, simply because it's two times two equals four. Oh, absurdity of absurdities! It's quite another thing to understand everything, to be conscious of everything, of all the impossibilities and stone walls; not to make peace with any of these impossibilities and stone walls if such peace disgusts you; to arrive by way of the most inevitable logical combinations at the most repulsive conclusions on the everlasting theme that you yourself are as if somehow to blame even for the stone wall, even though once again it's clearly obvious that you're in no way to blame; and as a consequence of this, while silently and impotently gnashing your teeth, to sink voluptuously into inertia, dreaming, as it turns out, that there's no one for you to be angry with, that you can find no object for your anger and perhaps will never find one, that it's all a magician's ruse, a stacked deck, a cardsharp's trick, simply a mess — you don't know what's what and who's who. But despite all these uncertainties and stacked decks, it still hurts inside you, and the less you know, the more it hurts!

IV

"Ha, ha, ha! After this, you'll be finding pleasure in a toothache!" you'll cry out with a laugh.

"And what of it? There's pleasure even in a toothache," I'll reply. Once, my teeth ached for a whole month; so I know there's pleasure in it. To be sure, in this case, people don't rage in silence; they moan; but the moans aren't sincere; they're spitefully fake moans, and the whole point is in the spiteful fakery. And it's precisely these moans that express the pleasure of the sufferer; if he didn't get pleasure from them,

4. There is a Russian proverb that says, "You can't break through a stone wall with your forehead." This proverb can be seen as representing the so-called truths of reason and prudence that the Underground Man is inveighing against. *Trans.*

he wouldn't be moaning. This is a good example, gentlemen, and I'm going to develop it. These moans express, first of all, the whole purposelessness of your pain, which your consciousness finds so humiliating; they express the whole lawfulness of nature, which you spit on, of course, but from which you nonetheless suffer, whereas she doesn't. They express the consciousness that you can't find an enemy here, but that nevertheless there is pain; the consciousness that, with all your possible Wagenheims,[5] you're totally enslaved to your teeth; that if somebody wants it, your teeth will stop hurting, but if he doesn't want it, they'll keep hurting for another three months; and that, finally, if you still disagree and keep protesting, the only consolation you'll have left is to flog yourself, or to slam your fist as painfully as possible against your wall, and absolutely nothing else. Well, sir, it's these bloody insults, these mockeries coming from who-knows-where, that finally give rise to a pleasure that sometimes reaches a point of extreme sensual delight. I ask you, gentlemen, to listen carefully sometime to the moans of an educated man of the nineteenth century who's suffering from a toothache, especially on the second or third day of his ailment, when he begins to moan quite differently than on the first day — that is, not simply because his teeth hurt, not like some rough peasant, but like a man touched by progress and European civilization, a man who has "detached himself from the soil and the popular roots,"[6] as the current saying goes. His moans become sort of vile and nastily angry, and they continue for whole days and nights. Yet he himself knows that his moans won't do him any good; he knows better than anyone else that he's only agitating and aggravating himself and others in vain; he knows that even the public before whom he's performing, and his whole family, are already listening to him with disgust, don't believe him for a second, and understand perfectly well that he could moan differently, more simply, without all these flourishes and cadenzas, and that he's only indulging himself because he's evil

5. A number of dentists named Wagenheim were practicing in Petersburg at the time, a fact that Dostoevsky's readers would presumably have been aware of. *Trans.*

6. This phrase is typical of the social polemics of the 1860s. *Trans.*

and malicious. Well, it's precisely in all these consciousnesses and shamefulnesses that the pleasure lies. "So, I'm disturbing you, piercing your hearts with my moans, keeping everyone in the house from sleeping. Well, don't sleep, then; you, too, should feel every minute that my teeth ache. For you I'm no longer a hero, as I tried to seem before; I'm just a nasty little man, a shitty worm. Well, so be it! I'm delighted you've figured me out. Are you sick of listening to my vile little moans? Well, be sick, then; here's an even nastier cadenza for you. . . ." So, you don't understand even now, gentlemen? No, it's obvious that one needs to reach an extreme point of development and consciousness before one can understand all the ins and outs of this kind of pleasure! You're laughing? I'm delighted. My jokes, gentlemen, are, of course, in bad taste, uneven, incoherent, full of self-mistrust. But, after all, that's because I don't respect myself. Can a man with consciousness have the slightest respect for himself?

V

Well, is it possible, is it possible for a man to have the slightest respect for himself if he attempts to find pleasure even in the very sense of his own humiliation? I'm not saying this now out of any kind of cloying repentance. And, in general, I could never bear to say, "Pardon me, Papa, I won't do it again" — not because it was something I couldn't say but maybe because I was all too capable of saying it, and in what a way! As if on purpose I used to get into trouble at times when I was as blameless as a newborn lamb. That was the disgusting part of it. At the same time, I would again be feeling a tenderness in my soul; I would be repenting, shedding tears, and, of course, deceiving myself, even though I wasn't pretending in the least. It was my heart that seemed to be playing disgusting tricks here. . . . Here, one couldn't even blame the laws of nature, even though it's the laws of nature that have been offending me constantly and more than anything else throughout my life. It's disgusting to remember all this now, and it was disgusting then too. After about a minute or so, I'd already be angrily thinking that all this — all these repentances, all these tender feelings, all these vows of rebirth — was a lie, a revolting lie, an affected lie. But you may ask, Why did I contort and torment myself that way? The answer is this: Because it was awfully boring just to sit there with my hands folded in my lap; and so I went into all those contortions. That's why. If you take a closer look at yourselves, gentlemen, you'll understand that that's how it is. I invented adventures for myself and authored my own life, in order to have at least some sort of life to live. How many times it happened that — well, for example, I'd get offended for no reason, on purpose; and at such times you yourself know that you're getting offended for no reason, that you're pretending, but you work yourself up to such a point that, in the end, you really do become offended. All my life, I've been driven to contort myself in this way, so that finally I lost control over myself. There were times when I compelled myself to fall in love; I even did this twice. And I really suffered, gentlemen — word of honor. In the depths of your soul, you don't believe you're suffering; you feel the mockery stirring within you; but nevertheless I did suffer, and in the most authentic, legitimate manner; I was jealous, I was beside myself. . . . And I did it all out of boredom, gentlemen, out of boredom; it was the inertia that crushed me. After all, the direct, legitimate, immediate fruit of consciousness is inertia — that is, a conscious sitting-with-your-hands-folded-in-your-lap. I already mentioned this above. I repeat, I repeat emphatically: All spontaneous people and men of action are active precisely because they're dumb and limited. How can one explain this? Here's how: As a result of their limitations, these men of action take the most immediate and secondary causes for the primary ones; they thus become convinced more swiftly and easily than others that they've found an indisputable foundation for their activity, and so they find peace, and after all, that's the main thing. After all, before you can begin to act, you first have to be perfectly at peace, and not have any lingering doubts. But, as for me, for example, how can I ever find peace? Where are the primary causes which can serve as my foundation? Where do I get them? I do thought-exercises, and consequently for me every primary cause immediately drags another cause even more primary in its wake, and so on, ad infinitum. Such is the essence of all consciousness and thought. Once again, this must be the laws of nature. What, finally, is the result? Why, the same thing. You might remember: A while ago I was talking about revenge. (You probably weren't paying attention.) I said: A man revenges himself because he finds justice in doing so. That means he's found a primary cause, a foundation — to wit: justice. And so he's found peace on all sides, and consequently he revenges himself calmly and successfully, being convinced that he's performing an honorable and just deed. But, as for me, I don't see any justice here; nor do I find any virtue; and, consequently, if I begin to revenge myself, it will be solely because I'm evil. The evil could, of course, overpower everything, all of my doubts; and it could therefore quite successfully take the place of a primary cause, precisely because it's not a cause. But what's to be done if there's not even any evil in me? (That's exactly where I began a while ago.) Again, as a consequence of these accursed laws of consciousness, the evil in me is subject to chemical decomposition. You look — and the object is volatilized, the reasons evaporate, the guilty party can't be found, the offense becomes not an offense but a *fatum*, something like a toothache, for which no one's to blame, and consequently you're left again with the same way out — that is, to beat your head against the wall even more painfully. And so, you wave at it dismissively because you haven't found a primary cause. But try letting yourself be carried away by your feelings, blindly, without reflection, without a primary cause, chasing away your consciousness at least for a period of time; try hating, or falling in love, just so you don't have to sit with your hands folded. The day after tomorrow, at the latest, you'll start despising yourself for having knowingly deceived yourself. The result: a soap bubble, and inertia. Oh, gentlemen, it may be that I consider myself an intelligent man only because, in the course of my entire life, I could neither begin nor end anything. Let it be the case, let it be the case that I'm a babbler, a harmless, irritating babbler, like all of us. But what is to be done if the direct and unique vocation of every intelligent man is babble — that is, the intentional pouring of water through a sieve?

VI

Oh, if it were only laziness that caused me to do nothing. Lord, how I'd respect myself then. I'd respect myself because I'd at least be capable of being lazy; I'd have at least one apparently positive quality, which I myself could be certain of. Question: Who are you? Answer: A lazy idler. Why, that would be very pleasant to hear about oneself. That would mean that I have a positive definition, that there's something that can be said about me. "Lazy idler!" That's a vocation and a mission; that's a career, gentlemen. No kidding — it's really true. By all rights that would make me a member of the best club in the land; and my sole occupation would be to respect myself continuously. I knew a certain gentleman who took pride all his life in being a connoisseur of Lafite. He regarded this as his positive virtue and never doubted himself. He died not merely with a peaceful conscience but even with a triumphant one, and he was perfectly right. And I would then have chosen a career for myself: I would have been a lazy idler and a glutton, though not an ordinary one, but one who, for example, sympathized with everything that is beautiful and sublime. How do you like that? I've long dreamt of that. This "beautiful and sublime" has weighed heavy on my head in the course of my forty years, but that's *my* forty years — whereas then, oh, then, things would have been different! I would have immediately found an appropriate activity for myself: namely, drinking the health of everything beautiful and sublime. I would have seized every occasion first to shed a tear into my glass and then to drain it in the name of everything that is beautiful and sublime. I would have transformed everything in the world into the beautiful and sublime; I would have found the beautiful and sublime in the nastiest, most indisputable crap. I would have exuded tears like a wet sponge. An artist, for example, has painted Ge's picture. I immediately drink the health of the artist who painted Ge's picture, since I love everything that is beautiful and sublime.[7] An au-

---

7. This is a reference to N. N. Ge's *The Last Supper* (exhibited in Petersburg in the spring of 1863), a painting Dostoevsky profoundly disliked. The Underground Man's raving about some artist who has painted Ge's picture is hard to make sense of, although it is undoubtedly an attack on Ge. *Trans.*

thor has written *As You Like It*;[8] and I immediately drink the health of "whoever you like" because I love everything that is beautiful and sublime. I'll demand to be respected for this; I'll persecute anyone who doesn't show me respect. I live peacefully, I die triumphantly — it's enchanting, utterly enchanting! And I'd have grown such a belly for myself then, fashioned for myself such a triple chin, developed such a ruby nose, that any passerby, looking at me, would have said, "That's a real plus! That's something really positive!" And, say what you will, it's very pleasant to hear such remarks in our negative age, gentlemen.

VII

But all this is golden dreams. Oh, tell me, who was the first to announce, the first to proclaim, that man does vile things only because he doesn't know his own true interests; and that if someone were to enlighten him and open his eyes to his true, normal interests, he would immediately stop doing vile things and immediately become good and honorable, because, being enlightened and understanding his own true profit, he would see his true profit precisely in the good, and everybody knows that no man can act knowingly against his own profit, and consequently he would, so to speak, necessarily start doing good? Oh, the child! Oh, the pure, innocent babe! But, in the first place, during all these millennia, when has man ever acted exclusively for his own profit? What is to be done with the millions of facts attesting that people *knowingly* — that is, completely understanding what their true profit is — have relegated this profit to the background and rushed headlong down a different path, one of risk and uncertainty, compelled by no one and nothing, but merely as if they didn't want to follow the prescribed path, and have stubbornly and willfully forged for themselves another path, an arduous and absurd one, seeking it almost in darkness? In

8. This is an attack on Dostoevsky's ideological opponent M. E. Saltykov-Shchedrin (1826-1889), who had published an article with this title in 1863. Saltykov-Shchedrin had also published an article praising Ge's *Last Supper. Trans.*

other words, this stubbornness and willfulness was really more agree-
able to them than any profit. . . . Profit! What is profit? And will you take
it upon yourself to define with perfect accuracy what man's profit consists in? But what if it happens that, *sometimes*, man's profit not only
can but even must consist precisely in desiring, in certain cases, not
what is profitable but what is harmful for him? But if that's so, if there
are such cases, the whole rule falls into dust. What do you think — are
there such cases? You're laughing; laugh away, gentlemen, but answer
the following question: Have man's profits been calculated with absolute certainty? Aren't there some profits which not only don't fit but
even can't be made to fit into any classification? You see, gentlemen, as
far as I know, you've taken your entire inventory of human profits as
averages from statistical data and from scientific-economic formulas.
You see, your profits comprise well-being, wealth, freedom, peace, and
so on and so forth, so that a man who, for example, openly and knowingly goes against this inventory would, in your view — and also in
mine, of course — be an obscurantist or an absolute madman. Isn't
that so? But here's the astonishing thing: How does it come about that,
in calculating man's profits, all these statisticians, all these sages and
lovers of the human race, constantly keep omitting one profit? They
don't even take it into account in that form in which it should be taken
into account, but the whole calculation depends on this. The problem
doesn't seem to be a very great one: just take it, this profit, and add it to
the list. But here's the rub: this peculiar profit doesn't fit into any classification and can't be added to any list. For example, I have a friend . . .
Gentlemen, I forgot! He's your friend, too, of course; whose friend isn't
he? Whenever he prepares for any undertaking, this gentleman immediately explains to you, pompously and clearly, precisely how he is re-
quired to act in accordance with the laws of reason and truth. As if
that's not enough, he'll talk to you excitedly and passionately about
true and normal human interests; with a mocking smile he'll reproach
the short-sighted simpletons who understand neither their own profit
nor the true meaning of virtue, and then — precisely a quarter of an
hour later, without any sudden, external cause, but simply because of
something inside him which is stronger than all his interests — he'll

completely reverse himself; that is, he'll act in obvious opposition to what he was just saying: in opposition to the laws of reason, in opposition to his own profit — well, in short, in opposition to everything. . . . Let me caution you: My friend is a collective person, and consequently one would find it hard to blame only him. The thing is, gentlemen, isn't there in fact something that almost every man finds more precious than his own maximum profit, or (so as not to violate logic) isn't there one maximally profitable profit (the omitted one we have just been speaking about) which is more important and more profitable than all other profits, and for the sake of which a man is ready, if necessary, to go against all laws, that is, to go against reason, honor, peace, well-being — in short, to go against all these beautiful and useful things, merely in order to attain this fundamental, maximally profitable profit which is more precious to him than all other things?

"But it's still profit, after all," you interrupt me. I beg your pardon, gentlemen, but I'll explain it all in a little while, and what matters here is not a play on words, but the fact that this profit is remarkable precisely because it does away with all of our classifications and constantly demolishes all the systems devised by the lovers of the human race for the happiness of the human race. In short, it interferes with everything. But before I name this profit, I want to compromise myself personally, and therefore I brazenly announce that all of these beautiful systems, all of these theories that aim to explain to humankind its true and normal interests in order that, necessarily striving to attain these interests, it would immediately become good and noble — these are, for the time being, in my opinion, mere logical exercises! Yes, gentlemen, logical exercises! After all, merely to maintain this theory of the renewal of the whole human race by means of a system of its own profits is, in my opinion, almost the same thing . . . as to maintain, for example, following Buckle,[9] that, as a result of civilization, man becomes softer and, consequently, less bloodthirsty and less capable of war. Logically, that does seem to follow from his arguments. But man has such a predi-

9. This is a reference to the thesis of the English historian Henry Thomas Buckle (1821-1862) in his *History of Civilization in England* (1857-1861). *Trans.*

lection for systems and abstract deductions that he's ready to distort the truth intentionally, to deny the evidence of his senses — to stop seeing and to stop hearing — merely to justify his logic. I'm taking this as an example because it's a particularly glaring example. Look around you: blood flows like a river, and in the merriest way, as if it were champagne. Take the whole of our nineteenth century, in which Buckle himself lived. Take Napoleon — both the great one and the present one.[10] Take North America — that eternal union.[11] Take, finally, the farce of Schleswig-Holstein.[12] And what is it that civilization softens in us? The only thing that civilization develops in man is a many-sidedness of sensations . . . and absolutely nothing else. And, through the development of this many-sidedness, man will perhaps reach a point where he finds pleasure in blood. In fact, this has already happened to him. Have you noticed that the most refined shedders of blood have almost always been the most civilized gentlemen to whom all these different Attilas and Stenka Razins[13] couldn't hold a candle, and if they're not as conspicuous as Attila and Stenka Razin, it's simply because we encounter them so often, because they're too ordinary and have become so familiar to us? In any case, if civilization hasn't made man more bloodthirsty, something has certainly made him more loathsomely, more disgustingly bloodthirsty than before. In the old days, man saw justice in bloodshed and, with a tranquil conscience, exterminated whomever it was necessary to exterminate; but nowadays, even though we consider bloodshed to be an abominable business, we keep persisting in this abomination, and now more than ever. Which is worse? Decide for yourselves. They say that Cleopatra (forgive the example from Roman history) liked to stick gold pins into the breasts of her slave-girls and took pleasure in their screams and writhings. You'll say that this oc-

10. This is a reference to Napoleon Bonaparte (1769-1821) and his nephew Napoleon III (1808-1873). *Trans.*

11. This is an ironic reference to the American Civil War. *Trans.*

12. At the time Dostoevsky was writing this, Prussia was at war with Denmark over possession of the duchy of Schleswig-Holstein. *Trans.*

13. Stenka Razin (?-1671) was a Cossack leader who led a bloody peasant uprising in Russia, which made him a popular hero. *Trans.*

curred in barbaric times, relatively speaking; that now, too, the times are barbaric, because (again, relatively speaking) pins are being stuck into breasts even now; that although man has now learned, on occasion, to see more clearly than in barbaric times, he's still far from having *learned* to act as reason and science would dictate. But nevertheless you're absolutely convinced that he'll be sure to learn to act correctly when he gets rid of certain old bad habits, and when common sense and science have completely re-educated human nature and turned it in a normal direction. You're convinced that man will then *voluntarily* stop making mistakes and will, so to speak, never willingly desire to set his will against his own normal interests. That's not all: then, you say, science itself will teach man (although, in my opinion, this is already a luxury) that in fact he doesn't have — and never has had — any will or caprice of his own, and that he himself is nothing more than something like a piano key or an organ stop;[14] and that, above that, the world also includes the laws of nature, so that everything he does is done not because he desires it, but of itself, according to the laws of nature. Consequently, we need only discover these laws of nature, and man will no longer have to answer for his actions, and it will be extremely easy for him to live. All human actions will then, of course, be computed on the basis of these laws, mathematically, like a table of logarithms up to 108,000, and entered in an index; or, better yet, certain well-meaning publications, like today's encyclopedic lexicons, will appear in which everything will be computed and defined with such exactitude that no more actions or adventures will be possible in the world.

At that time (it's still you talking) new economic relations will commence, ready-made and likewise calculated with mathematical precision, so that all possible questions will vanish instantaneously, simply because all possible answers will have been provided for them. Then, the crystal palace[15] will be erected. Then . . . Well, in short, we'll see the ar-

14. The metaphor of the piano key goes back to Diderot, who wrote in his *Conversation between D'Alembert and Diderot* (1769), "Our senses are piano keys upon which . . . nature plays." *Trans.*

15. This is a reference to the crystal palace described in a dream in the novel *What Is to Be Done?* (1863) by N. G. Chernyshevsky (1828-1889), a radical writer and philoso-

rival of the Kagan, the bird of happiness.[16] Naturally, there are no guarantees (this is me talking now) that, for example, things won't be awfully
boring then (since what is there to do when everything is computed according to a table?), but, on the other hand, everything will be extraordinarily rational and prudent. Of course, people can think up almost anything out of boredom! They might even stick gold pins into breasts out of
boredom, but that's still not a big deal. The bad thing (this is me talking
again) is that, for all I know, they might even be thankful for the gold
pins then. After all, man is stupid, phenomenally stupid. That is, even
though he's not really stupid at all, he's so ungrateful that you can't find
another being like him. As for me, I, for example, wouldn't be surprised
in the slightest if, suddenly, for no particular reason, in the midst of the
universal future rational well-being, some gentleman with an ignoble
or, rather, with a degenerate and mocking physiognomy were to appear
and, putting his hands on his hips, were to say to all of us: How about it,
gentlemen, why don't we knock all this rational well-being into smither-
eens with one swift kick, with the sole purpose of sending all these logarithms to the devil, and so that we could live again according to our own
stupid will! Again, none of this is a big deal, but the annoying thing is
that he'd be sure to find followers: that's how man is organized. And the
cause of this is the most foolish thing possible, something that seems
scarcely worth mentioning: people, always and everywhere, whoever
they might be, have always preferred to act as they desired and not at all
according to the dictates of reason and profit; and one's desire can be in
opposition to one's own profit, and sometimes it even *positively must* be
in opposition to it (this is now my idea). One's own voluntary and free desire, one's own caprice, even the craziest one, one's own fantasy, excited
sometimes to the point of madness — all this is in fact that very same
maximally profitable profit, the omitted one, which doesn't fit into any
classification and which constantly scatters all systems and theories to

---

pher who is the target of much of the satire in *Notes from Underground*; it is also a reference to the actual building designed by Sir Joseph Paxton and erected for the Great Exhibition in London in 1851. The Crystal Palace of the Great Exhibition became a symbol of
the new technological age. *Trans.*

16. The Kagan is the bird of happiness in Russian folklore. *Trans.*

the devil. And where did all these wise men get the idea that man needs some sort of normal or virtuous desire? What has made them necessarily imagine that man necessarily needs a rationally profitable desire? Man needs only his own *independent* desire, whatever this independence might cost and wherever it might lead. And as for desire, who the hell knows . . .

VIII

"Ha, ha, ha! But desire, in essence, if you will, doesn't even exist!" you interrupt me, laughing loudly. "Science has succeeded in anatomizing man to such an extent that we now know that desire and so-called free will are nothing more than . . ."

"Wait, gentlemen, that's exactly how I wanted to begin. I admit, I was even frightened. I was just about to shout who in hell knows what desire depends on, and that maybe thank God for that, but then I remembered science and . . . stopped dead in my tracks. And then you started talking. Well, actually, if some day they do in fact find some formula for all our desires and caprices — that is, a formula describing what they depend on, the precise laws that determine how they arise, how they multiply, what they're directed at in such and such a case, etc., etc. — that is to say, a real mathematical formula — then maybe man will immediately stop desiring; what's more, maybe he'll even definitely stop. Really, who would want to desire with reference to a mathematical table? As if that's not enough, he'll immediately be transformed from a man into an organ stop or something of the sort, because what is man without desires and without will if not an organ stop? What do you think? Let's calculate the probabilities — can this happen or not?"

"Hmm . . . ," you decide, "for the most part, our desires are erroneous because we have an erroneous view of our profit. We sometimes desire absolute nonsense because, owing to our stupidity, we see in this nonsense the easiest way to gain some profit we've decided on beforehand. Well, but when all this is analyzed and calculated on paper (which is perfectly possible, because, after all, it's vile and absurd to be-

lieve in advance that man will never discover certain laws of nature) —
then, of course, so-called desires will no longer exist. For if desire someday meshes perfectly with reason, we will then reason, and not desire,
simply because, after all, it would be impossible, for example, while re-
taining your reason, to *desire* absurdity and thus knowingly to oppose
reason and desire harm for yourself. . . . And since all desires and in-
stances of reasoning can in fact be calculated, because someday they'll
discover the laws of our so-called free will, then consequently, and all
kidding aside, it might be possible to construct something like a table so
that we would actually desire according to this table. For, if, for example, someday they do the calculations and prove to me that if I gave
someone the finger, it was precisely because I had to do it, and had to do
it exactly the way I did it, then what *freedom* is left me, especially if I'm a
learned man and have gotten a degree somewhere? Well, then I'd be
able to calculate my whole life thirty years in advance; in short, if
things were arranged that way, there would, after all, be nothing left for
us to do; we'd just have to accept things as they are. And, in general, we
have to repeat endlessly to ourselves that at such and such a moment
and in such and such circumstances, nature certainly doesn't ask our
permission; that we have to accept her as she is and not as we fantasize
about her; and if it's really our aspiration to be ruled by the table and
the formula, and, well . . . well, even by the test tube, there's nothing to
be done, then, we have to accept the test tube too! If not, it will be accepted without you. . . ."

Well and good, gentlemen, but at this point I've hit a snag! Forgive
me for all this philosophizing; that's what forty years of the underground will do to you! Allow me to fantasize. You see: reason, gentlemen, is a good thing; that's indisputable; but reason is only reason and
satisfies only man's rational faculty, whereas desire is a manifestation
of the whole of life — that is, of the whole of human life, including reason and including all the itches. And although our life, in this manifestation, often turns out to be nothing but crap, nevertheless it's life and
not just square-root extraction. After all, for example, it's perfectly natural that I desire to live in order to satisfy all my life faculties, and not
only my rational faculty — that is, not only some one-twentieth of all

my life faculties. What does reason know? Reason knows only what it has succeeded in learning (it may be that it will never learn some things; this may not be a consolation, but why not say it?), but man's nature acts as a whole, with everything that is in it, consciously and unconsciously; and even though it lies, it lives. I suspect, gentlemen, that you're regarding me with pity; you keep repeating to me that an enlightened and cultured man — such, in short, as the man of the future will be — cannot knowingly desire anything unprofitable for himself — that that's mathematics. I agree totally that it really is mathematics. But I repeat to you for the hundredth time: there is only one case, only one, when a man can intentionally and consciously desire for himself even what is harmful and stupid, even what is extremely stupid: namely, in order *to have the right* to desire for himself even what is extremely stupid and not be constrained by the obligation to desire for himself only what is intelligent. After all, this extremely stupid thing that we desire, this caprice of ours may, in fact, gentlemen, be for us the most profitable thing that exists on earth, especially in certain cases. And in particular it may be more profitable than all other profits even when it causes us obvious harm and contradicts the soundest conclusions of our reason regarding our profit — because, in any case, it preserves for us what is most important and most precious — that is, our personality and our individuality. Some, you see, maintain that this really is the most precious thing for man; desire can, of course, if it so desires, be in agreement with reason, especially if this is not abused but used in moderation; this is useful and sometimes even praiseworthy. But very often, and even for the most part, desire is utterly and stubbornly opposed to reason and . . . and . . . do you know, that too is useful and sometimes even very praiseworthy? Gentlemen, let us suppose that man is not stupid. (After all, it's really impossible to call him stupid, if only because if he's stupid, who's intelligent?) But even if he's not stupid, nevertheless he's monstrously ungrateful! Phenomenally ungrateful. I even think that the best definition of man is a two-legged being who is ungrateful. But that's still not all; that's still not man's worst defect; his worst defect is his constant depravity, constant from the time of the Great Deluge to the Schleswig-Holstein period of human destiny.

Depravity and, consequently, lack of good sense; for it's long been known that lack of good sense results from nothing else but depravity. Just cast a glance at the history of humankind — well, what do you see? Is it majestic? To be sure, some of it may be majestic; the Colossus of Rhodes alone, for example, counts for a great deal! After all, Mr. Anaevsky[17] is not just shooting the breeze when he reports that some say it's the work of man's hands, while others maintain that it was created by nature herself. Is it colorful? To be sure, perhaps it is colorful, too: if you consider only the full-dress uniforms, military and civilian, of all peoples in all ages — why, that alone is worth a great deal, and if you include the everyday uniforms, you'll never get to the end of it; no historian would be equal to the task.[18] Is it monotonous? Yes, perhaps it is monotonous: they fight and fight, and they're fighting even now, and they fought in the past, and they'll fight in the future — you have to agree that this is even too monotonous. In short, you can say anything at all about the history of the world — anything that might enter the head of the most disturbed imagination. The only thing one can't say is that it's rational. The very word sticks in one's throat. And here's the sort of thing we encounter all the time: such moral and rational people, such sages and lovers of the human race, are constantly turning up in life who make it their goal to live their entire lives as morally and rationally as possible, to be, so to speak, a light for their neighbors simply in order to demonstrate to them that it really is possible to live out one's life morally and rationally in the world. And so what? We know that many of these lovers of humanity, sooner or later, toward the end of their lives, have betrayed themselves, becoming involved in some unseemly story, sometimes even of the most indecent sort. Let me ask you now: What can one expect from man if he is a being endowed with such strange qualities? Shower him with all earthly blessings; submerge him in happiness over his head, so that only little bubbles pop up on the sur-

17. A. E. Anaevsky (1788-1866) was a critic whose articles were the object of much ridicule in the literary polemics of the period. *Trans.*

18. In Russia, after the Petrine reforms, uniforms were worn not only by military personnel but also by civil servants, who wore full-dress uniforms on special occasions as well as uniforms for everyday work. *Trans.*

face of happiness as if it were water; give him such economic prosperity that he'll have absolutely nothing left to do but sleep, eat cakes, and busy himself with the noncessation of world history — and even then, out of sheer ingratitude, out of sheer perversity, he — man, that is — would still do something vile. He'll even risk losing his cakes and deliberately desire the most pernicious rubbish, some absurdity that would ruin his economic prosperity, solely in order to inject his pernicious fantastic element into all this positive good sense. It's precisely his fantastic dreams, his vulgar stupidity, that he'll desire to retain, solely in order to confirm to himself (as if that were so very necessary) that people are still people, and not the keys of a piano on which the laws of nature threaten to play such a concerto that one won't be able to desire anything without referring to a mathematical table. But that's not all: even if man did in fact turn out to be a piano key, even if that were proved to him by means of the natural sciences and mathematically, he still wouldn't become reasonable but would deliberately do something perverse, out of sheer ingratitude, merely to have his own way. And if it turns out that he doesn't have the means, he'll think up destruction and chaos, he'll think up all sorts of sufferings, and still have his own way! He'll unleash a curse upon the world, and since only man can unleash curses (that's his privilege, the primary difference between him and the other animals), it may be, after all, that the curse alone will enable him to attain his object, which is to truly convince himself that he's a man and not a piano key! If you say that all this, too — the chaos, the darkness, the curse — can be calculated from a table, so that the mere possibility of calculating it beforehand will stop everything and enable reason to triumph — in that case, man will deliberately go insane in order to get rid of reason and have his own way! I believe in this, I answer for it, because, after all, the whole work of man really consists, it appears, in nothing but proving to himself every minute that he's a man, not an organ stop! It may be at the cost of his own skin, but he keeps proving it; it may be by cannibalism, but he keeps proving it. And after all this, how can one keep from sinning, from rejoicing that none of this has happened yet and that, for the time being at least, desire still depends on the devil knows what. . . .

You'll scream at me (if you still think me worthy of your screams) that no one's infringing on my free will; that they're merely busy arranging things in such a way that my will should, of its own free will, coincide with my normal interests, with the laws of nature and with arithmetic.

Good God, gentlemen, what sort of free will can there be when it all comes down to tables and arithmetic, when the only thing in play is two times two equals four? Two times two will equal four even without my will. As if that's what free will is!

IX

Gentlemen, I'm joking, of course, and I myself know that I'm joking ineptly, but, after all, not everything can be taken as a joke. I may be gnashing my teeth while I'm joking. Gentlemen, certain questions are torturing me; tell me what the answers are. Now, for example, you want to cure man of his old habits and reform his will in conformity with the demands of science and good sense. But how do you know that it's not only possible to reform man in that way but even *necessary* to reform him? What makes you conclude that human desire so necessarily *needs* to be reformed? In short, how do you know that such a reform will really be profitable for man? And, not to hold anything back, why are you so *absolutely* convinced that not to go against real, normal profit, guaranteed by the conclusions of reason and arithmetic, is in fact always so profitable for man and is a law for all humanity? After all, that's still only an assumption of yours. Let's suppose that it's a law of logic, but it may not be a law of humanity at all. You may be thinking, gentlemen, that I'm insane. Let me qualify what I've said. I agree: Man is preeminently a creative animal, predestined to strive consciously toward a goal and to engage in the engineering art — that is, to build a road for himself eternally and constantly, *wherever it may lead.* But sometimes he may want to deviate to the side precisely because he's *predestined* to build this road, and perhaps also because, however stupid the man of action may be in general, the thought will sometimes occur to him that

30

the road, as it turns out, almost always does go *somewhere, wherever that may be,* and that the main thing isn't where it goes but that it goes at all, and that the well-behaved child, neglecting the engineering art, shouldn't succumb to pernicious idleness, which, as we all know, is the mother of all the vices. Man loves to create, and to build roads; that's indisputable. But why does he also love destruction and chaos so passionately? Tell me that, if you can! But I'd like to say a couple of words about that myself. Isn't it possible that he loves destruction and chaos so passionately (after all, there's no disputing that sometimes he does love them very much; that's how it is) because he's instinctively afraid of attaining his goal and finishing the edifice he's building? How do you know — maybe he loves the edifice only from a distance, not from up close; maybe he only likes to build it, not to live in it, abandoning it afterwards *aux animaux domestiques,* such as ants, sheep, etc., etc. Now the ants have quite a different taste. They have an astonishing edifice of the same kind, forever indestructible — the anthill.

The supremely worthy ants began with the anthill, and most likely they'll end with the anthill, which does the greatest credit to their perseverance and good sense. But man is a thoughtless and unseemly being, and perhaps, like a chess player, he loves only the process of attaining the goal, not the goal itself. And who knows (there are no guarantees) — perhaps the sole goal on earth toward which humankind is striving consists merely in this continuous process of attaining the goal; in other words, it consists in life itself, and not really in the goal, which, of course, must be nothing other than two times two equals four — that is, a formula — and, after all, two times two equals four is no longer life, gentlemen, but the beginning of death. At least, man has always somehow been afraid of this two times two equals four; and as for me, I'm afraid of it now. Let us grant that the only thing man does is seek this two times two equals four; he traverses the oceans, sacrifices his own life in the quest; but to succeed, to actually find it — honest to God, he's somehow afraid. For he feels that as soon as he finds it, there'll no longer be anything to seek. When workers have finished their work, they at least receive their money, go to the tavern, and then end up in the police station — and that fills up their week. But where can man go? At any rate, one can observe something awkward about him every time he attains such a goal. He loves the process of attaining, but hardly likes the attainment, and that, of course, is awfully funny. In short, man is organized comically; there seems to be a kind of joke in all this. But, all the same, two times two equals four is an awfully insufferable thing. Two times two equals four — why, in my opinion, it's nothing but insolence, gentlemen. Two times two equals four is a cocky dude who stands with his hands on his hips, blocking your way and spitting at you. I agree that two times two equals four is a superb thing, but if we're to give everything its due, two times two equals five is sometimes a very splendid little thing too.

And why is it you're so firmly, so triumphantly convinced that only the normal and the positive — in short, only his well-being — is profitable for man? Perhaps reason is wrong when it comes to profit? After all, perhaps man loves not only his well-being. Perhaps he loves suffering just as much. Perhaps suffering is just as profitable for him as his well-being. And man sometimes loves suffering terribly, passionately; and that's a fact. And you don't need to consult world history here; if you're a man and have lived even a little bit, just ask yourself. As for my own personal opinion, I think it's even somewhat indecent to love only well-being. Whether it's good or bad, it's sometimes also very pleasant to demolish something. I'm not really in favor of suffering; nor am I in favor of well-being. I'm in favor . . . of my caprice, and of its being guaranteed to me when necessary. Suffering would be out of place in vaudevilles, for example; I know that. In a crystal palace it's even unthinkable; suffering is doubt, negation — what kind of crystal palace would it be if one could doubt in it? And yet I'm convinced that man will never renounce real suffering — that is, destruction and chaos. After all, suffering is the sole cause of consciousness. Even though I declared earlier that, in my opinion, consciousness is man's greatest misfortune, nevertheless I know that man loves it and wouldn't trade it for any satisfactions. Consciousness, for example, is infinitely higher than two times two. After two times two, there's of course nothing left to do or even to learn. The only thing left to do would be to bottle up your five senses and submerge yourself in contemplation. On the other hand, with consciousness, even though you get the same result — that is, even though there's still nothing to do — you can at least flog yourself sometimes, and that, at any rate, will enliven you. Reactionary as it is, it's still better than nothing.

X

You believe in some crystal edifice that is forever indestructible — that is, in an edifice you won't be able to stick out your tongue at on the sly or give the finger to in your pocket. Well, maybe I'm afraid of this edifice just because it's crystal and forever indestructible, and because you won't be able to stick out your tongue at it even on the sly.

Well, you see, if instead of a palace there was a henhouse, and it starting raining, I might crawl into it to keep from getting wet, but I still wouldn't take the henhouse for a palace out of gratitude, just because it protected me from the rain. You're laughing; you even say that in such circumstances a henhouse is just as good as a mansion. Yes, I answer, if the sole purpose of life were to keep from getting wet.

But what's to be done if I've gotten it into my head that that's not the only thing one lives for, and that if one is to live, one might as well live in a mansion? That's my desire; that's my wish. You'll scrape it out of me only when you change my desire. Well, change it then, seduce me with another one, give me another ideal. But until then I won't take the henhouse for a palace. Let it even be the case that the crystal edifice is an idle dream, that, according to the laws of nature, it shouldn't even exist, and that I've invented it solely as a consequence of my own stupidity, as a consequence of certain old-fashioned, irrational habits of our generation. But what business is it of mine that it shouldn't exist? Isn't it all the same if it exists only in my desires, or, to put it better, if it exists only as long as my desires exist? Perhaps you're laughing again? Laugh away; I'll put up with any mockery rather than say that I'm full when I want to eat; I know all the same that I won't be satisfied with a compromise, with a continuously recurring zero just because it exists according to the laws of nature and exists *in reality.* I won't accept as the crown of my desires an apartment building with rooms for poor tenants on a thousand-year lease and, for good measure, with a sign that says "Wagenheim, Dentist." Destroy my desires, eradicate my ideals, show me something better, and I'll follow you. Perhaps you'll say it's not worth the trouble; but in that case I can answer you in kind. We're having a serious discussion; but if you won't deign to give me your attention, I won't grovel before you. I have my underground.

But while I'm still alive and feel desire, let my hand wither[19] if I contribute even one little brick to such an apartment building! Never mind that I myself have just rejected the crystal edifice for the sole reason that you can't taunt it with your tongue. I said that not because I'm so fond of sticking out my tongue. Perhaps the only thing that made me mad was that, among all your edifices, there's still not a single edifice that one is not able to stick out one's tongue at. On the contrary, I'd let my tongue be cut off completely, out of sheer gratitude, if things could be arranged in such a way that I'd lose all desire to stick it out. What business is it of mine that it's impossible to arrange things that way and that it's necessary to be satisfied with an apartment building? Why, then, am I constituted with such desires? Can it be that I'm constituted this way simply in order to come to the conclusion that my entire constitution is a fraud? Can this be the whole goal? I don't believe it.

But you know what: I'm convinced that we, the underground men, must be kept on a leash. Although we're capable of sitting silently in the underground for forty years, once we come out into the light of day and let loose, we talk and talk and talk. . . .

XI

In the last analysis, gentlemen, it's better to do nothing! The best thing is conscious inertia! And so, long live the underground! Even though I said that I envy the normal man to the point of my bile spilling out of my throat, still I don't want to be him in the circumstances in which I

19. See Psalm 137:5. *Trans.*

see him (although, all the same, I won't stop envying him). No, no, the underground is, in any case, more profitable! There one can at least . . . Oh, but even now I'm lying! I'm lying because I myself know, like two times two, that it's not at all the underground that's better, but something different, totally different, for which I'm thirsting, but which I can't ever find! To hell with the underground!

It would even be better if I myself believed at least something of all the things I've just written. I swear to you, gentlemen, that I don't believe a word, not one little word, of all the things I've just scribbled! That is, I do believe it, perhaps, but at the same time, who knows why, I feel and suspect that I'm lying like a shoemaker.

"Then why did you write all of this?" you say to me.

And what if I lock you up in the underground for forty years with no occupation and then come back forty years later to see what's become of you? How can a man be left alone for forty years with nothing to do?

"But isn't that shameful, isn't that humiliating?" you'll perhaps say to me, shaking your heads contemptuously. "You thirst for life but try to resolve life's problems by means of a logical tangle. And how importunate, how insolent your outbursts are, and at the same time how scared you are! You talk rubbish and are pleased with it; you say impudent things but are constantly frightened by what you've said and keep apologizing. You keep assuring us that you're afraid of nothing, and at the same time you're trying to ingratiate yourself into our good opinion. You keep assuring us that you're gnashing your teeth, but at the same time you're trying to be witty so as to amuse us. You know your witticisms aren't witty, but you're obviously quite pleased with their literary quality. It's possible that you've really suffered, but you don't have any respect for your own suffering. There might be some truth in you but not a shred of modesty; out of the pettiest vanity you shamefully expose your truth in the marketplace. . . . You really want to say something, but you hide your final word out of fear, because you don't have the decisiveness to utter it, and have nothing but a cowardly insolence. You boast of consciousness, yet you do nothing but vacillate, because, even though your mind works, your heart is black with depravity, and with-

35

out a pure heart, there can be no full, genuine consciousness. And how importunate you are, constantly forcing yourself on others and twisting yourself into a pretzel! Lies, lies, lies!"

It goes without saying that all these words of yours have been written by me. That, too, is from the underground. For forty years in a row I've been listening to these words of yours through a little slit. I've thought them up myself, since that's the only thing I could think up. It's no wonder that I've learned them all by heart and that they've taken on a literary form. . . .

But can you really be — can you really be so credulous as to imagine that I would publish all this and then also give it to you to read? And here's another question for me: Why do I keep calling you "gentlemen"? Why do I keep addressing you as if you really were my readers? Such confessions as I intend to begin making here aren't published and aren't given to others to read. At least, I don't have enough strength for that, and I don't think it's necessary that I should have. But you see: a certain fantasy has entered my head, and I want to realize it at all costs. Here's what it's all about.

The memories of every man contain certain things he won't reveal to anyone, except perhaps to his friends. They also contain things he won't reveal even to his friends, but will reveal only to himself, and that in secret. And, finally, they contain things he's afraid to reveal even to himself; and every respectable man will have accumulated a fair number of such things. It even happens that the more respectable a man is, the more such things he has accumulated. At any rate, I myself have only recently decided to remember some of my past adventures; till now I've always avoided them, even with a certain anxiety. But now, when I'm not only remembering them but have actually decided to record them, I want to try the following experiment: Can one be perfectly honest even with oneself and not be afraid of the whole truth? Let me remark in parenthesis: Heine maintains that faithful autobiographies are almost impossible, and that a man is certain to lie about himself. In his opinion, Rousseau, for example, certainly told lies about himself in his confession, and even lied intentionally, out of vanity. I'm convinced that Heine's right; I understand very well how one can sometimes impute all sorts of crimes to oneself solely out of vanity, and I even know quite well what sort of vanity that might be. But Heine was making judgments about a man who confessed before the public. As for me, I'm writing only for myself, and let me declare once and for all that even if I'm writing as if I were addressing readers, that's only for show, because it's easier for me to write that way. It's a form, just an empty form; I'll never have any readers. I've already declared as much. . . .

I don't want to be constrained by anything in preparing my notes. I won't introduce any order or system. Whatever I remember, that's what I'll write down.

Now, for example, someone could nitpick at my words and ask me, If you're really not counting on having any readers, why are you making such agreements with yourself, and on paper no less, that you won't introduce any order or system, that you'll write whatever you remember, etc., etc.? Why are you explaining? Why are you apologizing?

"Well, that's how things sometimes turn out," I answer.

Anyway, there's a whole psychology here. And it may be that I'm just a coward. Or it may be that I'm deliberately imagining a public before me in order to behave more decently as I'm writing things down. There could be a thousand reasons.

But here's another thing: Why is it that I want to write? If it's not for the public, couldn't I simply recall it all in my own mind without translating it onto paper?

That's true, but yet it will turn out to be more imposing on paper. There's something more impressive about it; the judgment on oneself will be weightier; it will gain in style. Besides, maybe the writing will actually bring me some relief. Right now, for example, I'm particularly oppressed by a memory of something that happened long ago. I remembered it clearly a few days ago, and since then it's remained with me like an annoying tune that doesn't want to go away. And yet I have to get rid of it somehow. I have hundreds of such memories; but at times a single one stands out from those hundreds and oppresses me. For some reason I believe that if I write it down, it will go away. Why not try?

Finally: I'm bored, and I never do anything. And writing things down actually seems like work. They say work makes a man good and honest. Well, at least there's a chance.

Snow is falling now, an almost wet, yellow, dull snow. It was falling yesterday, too, and it was falling a few days ago. It think it was apropos of the wet snow that I remembered this episode which I can't get rid of now. And so let this be a tale apropos of the wet snow.

PART TWO

Apropos of the Wet Snow

When from dark error's subjugation
My words of passionate exhortation
Had wrenched thy fainting spirit free;
And writhing prone in thine affliction
Thou didst recall with malediction
The vice that had encompassed thee:
And when thy slumbering conscience, fretting
By recollection's torturing flame,
Thou didst reveal the hideous setting
Of thy life's current ere I came:
When suddenly I saw thee sicken,
And weeping, hide thine anguished face,
Revolted, maddened, horror-stricken,
At memories of foul disgrace.
Etc., Etc., Etc.

N. A. Nekrasov[1]

---

1. This is Juliet Soskice's translation of N. A. Nekrasov's poem (1845) about a rescued prostitute. *Trans.*

I

I was only twenty-four years old then. Even then my life was gloomy, disordered, and solitary to the point where I might as well have been living in the wilderness. I didn't see anyone, even avoided talking, and I buried myself more and more in my corner. When I was at work in the office, I even tried not to look at anyone, and I was perfectly well aware that my colleagues not only regarded me as an eccentric, but even looked at me — it always seemed to me — with a certain loathing. It used to come into my head: Why am I the only one who imagines that people are looking at him with loathing? One of my colleagues had a revolting, pock-marked face, which made him look like a robber. I probably wouldn't even have dared to look at anyone if I had such an indecent face. Another colleague had a uniform that was so worn that there was a bad smell emanating from him. Yet neither of these gentlemen showed the slightest embarrassment — either about his clothes or his face, or somehow morally. Neither one imagined that people were looking at him with loathing; and if either had so imagined, it wouldn't have mattered to him at all as long as it wasn't his supervisor who was doing the looking. It's perfectly clear to me now that, as a consequence of my infinite vanity and therefore of the high standard I set for myself, I very often looked at myself with a frenzied dissatisfaction verging on loathing, and for that reason, in my own mind, I attributed my view to everyone else. For example, I hated my own face; I found it to be foul, and even suspected that there was something vile in my expression, and therefore every time I arrived at work, I made an excruciating effort to behave as independently as possible, and to assume as noble an expression as possible, so that people wouldn't suspect me of being vile. "My face may be ugly," I thought, "but let it be noble, expressive, and, above all, *extremely* intelligent." But I knew with absolute and painful certainty that my face could never express all these perfections. But the most awful thing of all was that I found it to be positively stupid. I would have been fully reconciled to it if I could have looked intelligent. In fact, I would even have agreed to a vile expression if, at the same time, people had found my face to be strikingly intelligent.

Of course, I hated all of my colleagues, from first to last, and I despised them all, yet at the same time it was as if I was afraid of them. It happened that I would suddenly think they were superior to me. This would happen quite suddenly: I'd be despising them one minute and thinking they were superior to me the next. A cultivated and respectable man can't be vain without setting an infinitely high standard for himself, and without despising himself at certain moments to the point of self-hatred. But whether I despised them or thought them superior, I lowered my eyes almost every time I met anyone. I even conducted experiments — Could I endure so-and-so's gaze directed at me? — and I was always the first to lower my eyes. This tormented me to the point of madness. I also had a morbid fear of being ridiculous, and therefore I slavishly worshiped routine in all outward things; I loved to fall into the common rut, and with all my soul I was afraid of any eccentricity in myself. But how could someone like me carry this through? I was morbidly refined, as befits a man of our age. Whereas they were all dull-witted, and resembled one another as so many sheep in a flock. Perhaps I was the only one in the whole office who constantly imagined that I was a coward and a slave, and I imagined that precisely because I was refined. But it was not only that I imagined it; it really was so in fact: I *was* a coward and a slave. I say this without any embarrassment. Every respectable man of our time is and must be a coward and a slave. That's his normal condition. I'm profoundly convinced of that. That's how he's made and that's what he's constituted for. And a respectable man must be a coward and a slave not only at the present time, owing to some accidental circumstances, but generally in all periods of time. That's a law of nature for all respectable people on earth. If, on occasion, any one of them does happen to be brave in the face of something or other, he shouldn't be comforted or carried away by that; he'll be cowardly in the face of something else. That's the unique and eternal outcome. Only asses and mules are brave, and even then only up to a certain wall. It's not worth paying any attention to them, because they're of absolutely no significance.

One other circumstance tormented me at that time: no one else was like me, and I wasn't like anyone else. "I am one, but they are *all*," I would think, and then became lost in my thoughts.

From all of this you can see that I was still practically an adolescent.

The exact opposite would also occur. Sometimes the very idea of going to the office disgusted me; things would reach such a point that I often went home sick. But suddenly, for no particular reason, there would come upon me a phase of skepticism and indifference (everything happened in phases to me); and I would laugh at my intolerance and fastidiousness, and reproach myself for my *romanticism.* Usually I didn't want to talk to anyone, but at these times I would not only talk up a storm but would even contemplate making friends with my colleagues. All my fastidiousness would suddenly disappear for no rhyme or reason. Who knows? Maybe I never really had any fastidiousness, and it was just something put on, something borrowed from books. To this very day I still haven't answered that question. Once I even really did become friendly with them, began to visit their homes, to play a game of preference,[2] to drink vodka with them, to talk about promotions. . . . But, here, permit me to make one digression.

We Russians, speaking generally, have never had any of those stupid transcendental romantics — German, and especially French — on whom nothing produces any effect; even if the earth crumbled under them, even if all of France perished at the barricades, they'd still remain the same, they wouldn't change even for the sake of decency, but would go on singing their transcendental songs to the hour of their death, so to speak, because they're fools. We, in our Russian land, don't have any fools — everybody knows that. That's what distinguishes us from foreign and German lands. Consequently, we don't have these transcendental natures in their pure state. It was our "positive" journalists and critics of the time, hunting for the Kostanzhoglos and the Uncle Pyotr Ivanoviches[3] and foolishly accepting them as our ideal, who slandered our romantics, taking them for the same transcendental type as in Germany or France. On the contrary, the characteristics of our romantics are absolutely and directly opposed to the transcendental European

2. This was a card game popular at the time. *Trans.*

3. These two fictional characters exemplify practical acumen and good sense. Kostanzhoglo is a character in the second volume of Gogol's *Dead Souls* (1842). Uncle Pyotr Ivanovich is a character in Ivan Goncharov's novel *A Common Story* (1847). *Trans.*

type, and no European standard can be applied to them. (Do allow me to make use of this word "romantic" — an old-fashioned, much-honored little word which has done good service and is familiar to everyone.) What characterizes our romantics? They understand everything, *see everything, and often see it incomparably more clearly than our most positive minds do;* they refuse to make peace with anyone or anything, but at the same time they despise nothing; they get around everything, yield to everything, are politic with everyone; they never lose sight of useful and practical goals (such as a nice little apartment at government expense, a nice little pension, a nice little decoration); they keep an eye on these goals through all their enthusiasms and all their little volumes of lyrical verse, and at the same time they preserve "the beautiful and the sublime" inviolate within themselves to the hour of their death, and, by the way, they quite successfully preserve themselves too, like some precious jewels wrapped in cotton, if only, for example, for the benefit of that very same "beautiful and sublime." Our romantics are men of great breadth and the greatest rogues of all our rogues, I can assure you of that . . . even from my personal experience. Of course, if they're intelligent, that is. But what am I saying! Our romantics are always intelligent, and I only meant to observe that although we have had romantics who were fools, that doesn't count, simply because while still in the bloom of life, they completely degenerated into Germans, and to preserve their precious jewel more comfortably, they settled somewhere over there, usually in Weimar or in the Black Forest. I, for example, genuinely despised my work in the office, and if I didn't spit at it all, it was solely out necessity, because all I did was sit there and get money for that. As a result, please take note, I refrained from spitting. Our romantics would sooner go insane (a thing, however, which happens very rarely) than start spitting, unless they have another career in view; and they're never kicked out; at most, they're hauled off to the lunatic asylum like "the king of Spain,"[4] and that would happen only if they go completely insane. But it's only the weaklings and the fair-haired

---

4. This is a reference to what happened to the protagonist of Gogol's story "Diary of a Madman" (1835). *Trans.*

momma's boys who go insane in our country. Whereas an enormous number of romantics later attain significant rank. Their many-sidedness is extraordinary! And what a capacity they have for the most contradictory sensations! I used to be comforted by this thought even in those days, and I'm of the same opinion now. That's why there are so many "broad natures" among us who never lose their ideal even in the depths of degradation; and even though they would never lift a finger for their ideal, even though they're incorrigible thieves and rogues, yet they tearfully cherish their original ideal and are extraordinarily honest at heart. Yes, gentlemen, it's only among us that the most incorrigible rogue can be absolutely and even sublimely honest at heart without in the least ceasing to be a rogue. I repeat, time and again our romantics become such accomplished rascals (I use the word "rascals" affectionately), and suddenly display such a sense of reality and practical knowledge, that their bewildered superiors and the general public can only hang their tongues out in amazement.

Their many-sidedness is truly bewildering, and God only knows what it may develop into as circumstances change, and what it promises to bring us in the future. And the material, gentlemen, is not too shabby! I'm not saying this out of some ridiculous patriotism or jingoism. However, I'm sure that once again you must think I'm joking. But, who knows, maybe it's just the opposite, and you're sure that this is what I really think. In any case, gentlemen, I'll consider both of your opinions as an honor and a particular pleasure. But do forgive me my digression.

Of course, I didn't maintain the friendly relations with my colleagues, and we were soon spitting at each other; and as a consequence of what was still my youthful inexperience, I even stopped greeting them with a nod, which was a sign that I was cutting off relations. All this, however, only happened to me once. In general, I was always alone.

At home, to begin with, I spent most of my time reading. There was a desire to use external sensations to stifle all that was continuously seething inside me. And of all external sensations, the only one I had at my disposal was reading. Reading helped a lot, of course — it agitated, delighted, and tormented me. But at times it bored me fearfully. There was still a desire for movement, and I would suddenly plunge into dark, vile, subterranean vice — no, not into vice, but into a little vice-let, into a little debauchery. My nasty little passions were made sharp and burning by my constant morbid irritability. I experienced hysterical fits, with tears and convulsions. I had nowhere to go except into my reading — that is, there was nothing in my surroundings which I could respect then and which attracted me. What's more, I was beset by an anguished longing; there would come upon me a hysterical thirst for contradictions and contrasts, and so I'd plunge into vice. I've confessed all this not in order to justify myself . . . But, no! I'm lying! I precisely did want to justify myself. I made that tiny little observation for my own benefit, gentlemen. I don't want to lie. I gave my word I wouldn't.

I indulged in vice in solitude, by night, furtively, fearfully, filthily, with a feeling of shame which never deserted me, even at the most loathsome moments, and which at such moments took on all the dimensions of a curse. Even then I was carrying my underground in my soul. I was terribly afraid of somehow being seen, encountered, recognized. I wandered about in various very dark places.

Once one night as I was walking past some wretched little tavern, I looked through the lighted window and saw that some gentlemen were fighting with billiard cues and that one of them was being thrown out the window. At some other time this would have disgusted me, but at that moment my mood was such that I envied the gentleman who was thrown out the window, envied him so much that I even went into the tavern and into the billiard room. "Perhaps," I thought, "I'll get into a fight, too, and they'll throw me out the window."

I wasn't drunk — but what is one to do: Anguish can drive a man to such a pitch of hysteria! But nothing happened. It turned out I wasn't even capable of being thrown out the window, and I went away without fighting.

Some officer put me in my place as soon as I set foot inside.

I was standing by the billiard table and inadvertently blocking his way as he was trying to get by; so he took hold of me by my shoulders and silently — without any warning or explanation — moved me from where I was standing to another place and went past as though he hadn't noticed me. I could have forgiven even a beating, but there was no way I could forgive his moving me out of the way while entirely failing to notice me.

The devil knows what I would have given for an authentic quarrel, a more correct and decent one, a more *literary* one, so to speak! I had been treated like a fly. This officer was a good six feet tall, and I'm short and emaciated. However, the quarrel was in my hands; all I had to do was protest, and they certainly would have thrown me out the window. But I changed my mind and preferred . . . to beat a resentful retreat.

I left the tavern embarrassed and agitated, and went straight home, and the next day I continued my little vice-let still more timidly, more abjectly, more miserably than before, as if with tears in my eyes — but I continued it nonetheless. Don't think, though, that it was cowardice that made me slink away from the officer; I've never been a coward at heart, although I've always been a coward in action; but — don't be in a hurry to laugh. I have an explanation for this; rest assured, I have an explanation for everything.

Oh, if only that officer had been the kind who would consent to fight a duel! But no, he was one of those gentlemen (alas, long extinct!) who preferred fighting with billiard cues or, like Gogol's Lieutenant Pirogov,[5] appealing to the police. They didn't fight duels and, in any case, would have considered it unseemly to fight a duel with someone like me, a lowly civilian; and in general they would have considered a duel something inconceivable, something free-thinking and French, whereas they were quite ready to bully, especially when they were a good six feet tall.

I retreated not because of cowardice, but because of my absolutely unlimited vanity. I wasn't afraid of his six feet of height, or of receiving a painful beating and being thrown out of the window. I would have had enough physical courage for that; but I didn't have enough moral courage. I was afraid that none of those present, from the insolent marker down to the last putrid, pimply-faced, greasy-collared little

---

5. Lieutenant Pirogov is a character in Gogol's story "Nevsky Prospect" (1835). *Trans.*

clerk who was fluttering about there, would understand, but that, instead, they would all laugh at me when I began to protest and to address them in literary language. Because, to this very day, it's impossible among us to speak of a point of honor — that is, not of honor itself, but of a point of honor *(point d'honneur)* — except in literary language. You can't allude to a "point of honor" in ordinary language. I was fully convinced (a sense of reality, in spite of all my romanticism!) that they would all simply split their sides laughing, and that the officer, instead of giving me a simple beating — that is, an inoffensive one — would certainly knee me in the back, propelling me in this manner around the billiard table, and only then perhaps have pity on me and throw me out the window. Naturally, this couldn't be the end of this miserable story. Afterwards I often encountered that officer in the street and observed him very attentively. But I don't know whether he recognized me or not. He probably didn't; I deduced that from certain signs. As for me, I looked at him with anger and hatred, and it continued this way . . . for several years, gentlemen! My anger grew even stronger and increased as the years passed. At first I began making stealthy inquiries about this officer. This was difficult for me, since I didn't know anybody. But once I heard someone call him by his surname in the street while I was walking behind him at some distance as if tied to him — that's how I learned his name. Another time I followed him all the way back to his apartment building, and for ten kopecks learned from the caretaker where he lived, on what floor, whether he lived alone or with someone, etc. — in short, everything one could learn from a caretaker. Then one morning, although I had never tried my hand at literature, it suddenly came into my head to write a description of this officer as an exposé or caricature in the form of a story. I wrote the story with relish. I exposed him, I even slandered him a little; at first I altered his name in such a way that it could easily be recognized, but on second thought I changed it, and then sent the story to the *Notes of the Fatherland*.[6] But at that time such exposés weren't in fashion yet, and they didn't publish my story. That really annoyed me. Sometimes my anger positively choked me. Finally, I

6. This was a leading literary magazine founded in 1839. *Trans.*

47

decided to challenge my enemy to a duel. I composed a beautiful, charming letter to him, imploring him to apologize to me, and hinting rather plainly at a duel in case of his refusal. The letter was composed in such a way that if the officer had possessed the slightest understanding of "the beautiful and the sublime," he would certainly have come running to me, to fling himself on my neck and offer me his friendship. And how good that would have been! We would have gotten on so well together! He would have protected me with his rank, and I would have ennobled him with my culture, and, well . . . with my ideas, and who knows what might have come of all this? But imagine, this was already two years after he had insulted me, and my challenge would have been the most absurd of anachronisms, despite all the ingenuity of my letter in explaining away and disguising the anachronism. But, thank God (to this day I thank the Almighty with tears in my eyes), I didn't send the letter to him. Cold shivers run down my back when I think of what might have happened if I had sent it. Then suddenly . . . suddenly I revenged myself in the simplest way, by a stroke of genius! A brilliant idea suddenly came to me. Sometimes on holidays I used to stroll along the sunny side of the Nevsky Prospect[7] between three and four in the afternoon. That is, I didn't stroll at all, but rather experienced innumerable torments, humiliations, and attacks of bile; but that's probably what I needed. I used to wriggle along like an eel between the passersby, in a most unseemly fashion, constantly moving aside to make way for generals, for cavalry officers and hussars, or for young ladies; at those moments I used to feel convulsive pains in my heart and a burning down my back at the mere thought of the wretchedness of my attire, of the wretchedness and banality of my scurrying little figure. This was a regular martyrdom, a constant intolerable humiliation from the thought, which would turn into a constant and direct sensation, that I was a mere fly in the eyes of this whole world, a foul, obscene fly — more intelligent, more highly developed, more noble than everyone else, of course, but nonetheless a fly that was constantly making way for everyone, insulted and injured by everyone. Why did I inflict this torment

7. Nevsky Prospect is the main boulevard of Petersburg. *Trans.*

upon myself? Why did I stroll on Nevsky? I don't know. I was simply *drawn* there at every possible opportunity.

At that time I had already begun to experience surges of the pleasures I spoke about in the first chapter. After the story with the officer, I was even more strongly drawn there: it was on Nevsky that I encountered him most frequently; it was also there that I admired him. He, too, went there chiefly on holidays. He, too, moved aside for generals and persons of high rank, and he, too, wriggled between them like an eel; but he would simply trample people like me or those even slightly superior; he would walk straight at them as if there was nothing but empty space in front of him, and never, under any circumstances, would he turn aside. I reveled in my anger watching him and . . . angrily made way for him every time. It tormented me that even in the street I couldn't be on an equal footing with him. "Why must you always be the first to move aside?" I kept asking myself in hysterical rage, waking up sometimes at three in the morning. "Why always you and not he? After all, there's no law that says it must be that way; it's not written down anywhere, is it? Why can't we be on an equal footing, the way refined people usually are when they encounter each other? He moves aside halfway, and you move aside halfway; and both of you pass with mutual respect." But that never happened: I was always the one to move aside, while he didn't even notice that I made way for him. But suddenly an astonishing thought came into my head! "What if," I thought, "what if I encounter him and . . . don't move aside? What if I don't move aside on purpose, even if I have to bump into him? What would happen then?" Little by little this daring idea possessed me to such an extent that it gave me no peace. I dreamt about it constantly, horribly, and I purposely went more frequently to Nevsky to picture more clearly how I would do it when I did do it. I was in ecstasy. This intention seemed more and more probable and possible to me. "Of course, I won't bump into him hard," I thought, already becoming more good-natured in my joy. "I just won't turn aside. I'll bump into him a little bit, not very violently, but just touching shoulders, only as much as decency permits, so that I'll push him only as much as he pushes me." At last I made up my mind completely. But the preparations took a lot of time. To begin with, when I carried out my plan I would need to look rather more decent, and so I had to think of what to wear. "Just in case, if, for example, there's any sort of public scandal (and the public there is *superflu:*[8] a countess strolls there; Prince D. strolls there; the entire literary world is there), I have to be well-dressed; that would inspire respect and would, in a certain fashion, put us on an equal footing in the eyes of high society." With that goal in mind I asked for some of my salary in advance, and bought a pair of black gloves and a respectable hat at Churkin's store. Black gloves seemed to me both more dignified and more *bon ton* than the lemon-colored ones which I had contemplated at first. "The color is too gaudy — it looks as though one were trying to be conspicuous," and I didn't take the lemon-colored ones. I had already long beforehand prepared a good shirt, with white bone cufflinks; my overcoat was the only thing that held me back. In and of itself the overcoat was a very good one; it kept me warm; but it was wadded and it had a raccoon collar which was the height of vulgarity. I had to change the collar at all costs, and to get a beaver one of the sort that officers wear. For this purpose I began going to the Gostiny Arcade,[9] and after several attempts I set my sights on a cheap German beaver. These German beavers soon become worn and look wretched, yet at first, when they're brand-new, they look more than decent, and I only needed it for this one occasion. I asked the price; even so, it was expensive. After thinking it over thoroughly, I decided to sell my raccoon collar. The rest of the money, a considerable sum for me, I decided to borrow from Anton Antonych Setochkin, my immediate superior, a modest person, though serious and judicious. He never lent money to anyone, but, on entering the civil service, I had been specially recommended to him by the important personage who had secured the position for me. My torments were horrible. To borrow money from Anton Antonych seemed to me monstrous and shameful. I didn't even sleep for two or three nights, and in general I was sleeping little at that time; I was in a fever; I would feel a kind of vague sinking in my heart, or it would suddenly start jumping, jumping, jumping! . . . Anton

8. *Superflu* is French for "ultra-refined" — here used sarcastically. *Trans.*

9. This is a covered shopping arcade in the center of Petersburg. *Trans.*

Antonych was astonished at first, then he frowned, then he reflected; but in the end he did lend me the money, receiving from me a written authorization to deduct the sum advanced from my salary two weeks later. This way everything was finally ready; the handsome beaver was enthroned in place of the mangy raccoon, and I gradually began to get to work. One couldn't just do the thing at once, haphazardly; one had to do it methodically, step by step. But I must confess that after multiple attempts I even began to despair: it was simply impossible to collide with him! I made every preparation, and I was quite determined, but every time it seemed there would be a collision, I'd look around — and once again I'd stepped aside for him and he'd passed by without noticing me. I even used to pray as I approached him that God would grant me resolve. Once I was absolutely resolved to do it, but it ended in my falling under his feet because, at the very last instant, when I was only a few inches away from him, my courage failed me. He very calmly walked over me, and I bounced to one side like a ball. That night I was ill again, feverish and delirious. Then, suddenly, everything ended in the best possible way. The night before, I had conclusively made up my mind not to carry out my fatal plan and to abandon it all, and with that aim I went to Nevsky one last time, simply in order to see how I would abandon it all. Suddenly, three paces from my enemy, I unexpectedly made up my mind: I closed my eyes, and we collided solidly, shoulder against shoulder! I didn't yield an inch and passed him on a perfectly equal footing! He didn't even look back and pretended not to notice the collision; but he was only pretending — I'm convinced of that. I'm convinced of that to this day! Of course, I got the worst of it: he was stronger, but that wasn't the point. The point was that I had attained my goal, preserved my dignity, yielded not a step, and placed myself publicly on an equal social footing with him. I returned home fully avenged for everything. I was in ecstasy. I was triumphant and sang Italian arias. Of course, I won't describe to you what happened to me three days later; if you've read my first chapter, "The Underground," you can guess for yourself. Afterwards, the officer was transferred somewhere; I haven't seen him now for some fourteen years. I wonder what he's doing now, that dear friend of mine? Who's he trampling now?

II

But the phase of my little debauch, my vice-let, would end, and I'd become horribly nauseated. Repentance would come; I'd chase it away: it was too nauseating. Gradually, however, I grew used to that, too. I got used to everything — that is, it wasn't that I got used to it, but that I somehow voluntarily consented to endure it. But I had a way out that could reconcile everything: I could take refuge in "everything that was beautiful and sublime," in dreams, of course. I was an awful dreamer; I'd dream for three months in a row, hidden in my corner, and, believe me, in those moments I didn't resemble the gentleman who, in the agitation of his chicken heart, had sewn a German beaver onto the collar of his overcoat. I'd suddenly become a hero. I wouldn't have received my six-foot lieutenant then even if he had called on me to pay me a visit. I couldn't even picture him in my imagination then. What were my dreams, and how could I find satisfaction in them? That's hard to say now, but at the time I did find satisfaction in them. Besides, even now I'm finding satisfaction in them to some extent. My dreams were always sweeter and more powerful after my little debaucheries; they arrived with repentance and tears, with curses and ecstasies. There were moments of such positive intoxication, of such happiness, that I didn't even feel the slightest trace of mockery inside me, honest to God. I had faith, hope, love. That's the thing: I blindly believed then that, by some miracle, by some external circumstance, all this would suddenly open out, expand; that suddenly a horizon of suitable activity would appear, of activity that was beneficent, beautiful, and, above all, *quite ready-made* (I never knew what sort of activity, but the main thing was that it would be quite ready-made); and that I would suddenly step out into God's world, practically riding a white horse and crowned with laurel. I couldn't conceive of a secondary role for myself, and that's precisely why, in reality, I quite calmly accepted the last role. Either hero or dirt — there was nothing in between. That's what ruined me: when I was rolling in the dirt, I comforted myself with the thought that at other times I was a hero, and the hero was a cloak for the dirt: for an ordinary man, I thought, it was shameful to be dirtied, but a hero was too lofty to become entirely dirty, and consequently it was permissible for him to dirty himself. It's remarkable that I experienced these incursions of "everything that was beautiful and sublime" even during my little debauches and exactly when I was on the very bottom; these incursions came in separate bursts, as if reminding me of themselves, but they wouldn't put an end to my little debauch; on the contrary, they seemed to enliven it by contrast, and were only sufficiently present to serve as an appetizing sauce. That sauce consisted of contradictions and sufferings, of excruciating inner analysis; and all these torments and little agonies imparted a certain piquancy, even a certain meaning, to my little debauch; in short, they perfectly fulfilled the function of an appetizing sauce. All this was not without a certain profundity. Could I have really agreed to the simple, vulgar, direct little debauchery of an ordinary clerk and endured having all this dirt on myself? What was it in this dirt that could seduce me and lure me into the streets at night? No, gentlemen, I had a noble loophole for everything. . . .

But how much love, Lord, how much love I'd experience at times in those dreams of mine, in those "flights into everything that was beautiful and sublime"; although it was fantastic love, although it was never really applicable to anything human, there was so much of it, of this love, that later, in reality, I didn't even feel the need to apply it: that would have been a superfluous luxury. Everything, however, always concluded most satisfactorily with a lazy and intoxicating transition to art — that is, to beautiful forms of existence, quite ready-made, largely stolen from poets and novelists and adapted to all possible needs and uses. For example, I triumph over everyone; everyone, of course, is left in the dust and compelled to voluntarily recognize all my perfections, and I forgive them all. I fall in love, being a famous poet and a grand gentleman; I obtain countless millions and donate them immediately to humanity, and at the same time I confess before all the people my shameful deeds, which, of course, are not merely shameful, but include an extraordinary quantity of "the beautiful and the sublime," something in the style of Manfred.[10] Everyone weeps and kisses me (what idi-

10. This is the romantic hero of Byron's poetic tragedy *Manfred* (1817). *Trans.*

ots they would be if they didn't), while I go about barefoot and hungry, preaching new ideas and demolishing the reactionaries at Austerlitz.[11] Then the band plays a march, an amnesty is declared, and the pope agrees to leave Rome and go to Brazil;[12] then there's a ball for all of Italy at the Villa Borghese on the shores of Lake Como,[13] since Lake Como has intentionally been moved for that purpose to Rome; then there's a scene in the bushes, etc., etc. — as if you didn't know all about it. You'll say that it's vulgar and vile to drag all this into the marketplace now, after all the raptures and tears to which I've confessed. But why is it vile? Do you really think that I'm ashamed of all this, or that it's more stupid than anything in your own lives, gentlemen? Besides, I can assure you that some of these fantasies were by no means badly composed. . . . Not everything happened on the shores of Lake Como. And yet you're right: it really is vulgar and vile. And the vilest thing is that I've now begun to justify myself in your eyes. And viler still is the fact that I'm now making this remark. But that's enough, or there'll be no end to it: each thing will be viler than the last. . . .

I was never able to dream for more than three months in a row; after that I'd begin to feel an irresistible urge to plunge into society. For me, to plunge into society meant to visit my department chief, Anton Antonych Setochkin. He was the only permanent acquaintance I have ever had in my life, and I wonder at the fact myself now. But him too I went to see only when that urge came over me, and when my dreams had reached such a point of bliss that I felt an immediate and unfailing need to embrace my fellows and all of humankind; and for that purpose I needed at least one human being who actually existed. However,

11. Austerlitz is the site of Napoleon's great victory in December 1805 over the combined armies of two "reactionary" rulers: Tsar Alexander I of Russia and the Austrian emperor Francis II. *Trans.*

12. This is probably a reference to Napoleon's annexation of the papal states to France in 1809, after which he was excommunicated by Pope Pius VII. Napoleon held the pope captive for five years, although not in Brazil. *Trans.*

13. This is evidently a reference to the 1806 celebration of the founding of the French empire. The Villa Borghese, built in 1615 as a summer house on the outskirts of Rome, belonged in 1806 to Camillo Borghese, who was married to Napoleon's sister Paulina. Lake Como is situated in the Italian Alps. *Trans.*

one could call on Anton Antonych only on a Tuesday (his at-home day); consequently, I always had to adapt to Tuesday my need to embrace all of humankind. This Anton Antonych lived on the fourth floor in a house in Five Corners,[14] in four low-ceilinged rooms, one smaller than the other, of a particularly frugal and yellowish appearance. Living with him were his two daughters and their aunt, who would pour out the tea. One of the daughters was thirteen and the other fourteen, and both had snub noses. I was terribly embarrassed in their presence because they were always whispering and giggling together. The master of the house usually sat in his study on a leather couch in front of the table, together with some gray-headed visitor, usually a colleague from our office or even from some other department. I never saw more than two or three visitors there, always the same ones. They talked about excise taxes, about business in the Senate, about salaries, about promotions, about His Excellency, about ways of making oneself liked, etc., etc. I had the patience to sit like a fool beside these people for four hours at a stretch, listening to them without daring to talk to them or knowing what to say. I'd become stupefied; a few times I'd start perspiring; I'd be overcome by a sort of paralysis; but this was good and useful. On returning home I'd postpone for a while my desire to embrace all of humankind.

However, I did have one other acquaintance of a sort — Simonov, a former schoolmate of mine. No doubt I had many schoolmates in Petersburg, but I didn't associate with them and had even stopped nodding to them in the street. It may be that I had even transferred to another department in order to avoid their company and to cut off all at once all connection with my hated childhood. Curses on that school and on all those terrible years of penal servitude! In short, I parted from my schoolmates as soon as I was set free. There remained two or three to whom I still nodded in the street. One of them was Simonov, who had in no way been distinguished at school, and was even-tempered and quiet, but I detected in him a certain independence of character and even honesty. I

14. The Five Corners square is in the historic district of Petersburg near Nevsky Prospect. *Trans.*

don't even think he was particularly stupid. I had at one time spent some rather soulful moments with him, but these had not lasted long and had somehow been suddenly clouded over. Evidently he was burdened by these recollections, and was, it appeared to me, always afraid that I might lapse into the former tone. I suspected that he found me quite repulsive, but I still used to visit him, not being quite certain of it.

And so once, on a Thursday, unable to endure my solitude and knowing that on Thursdays Anton Antonych's door would be locked, I remembered Simonov. Climbing up to his fourth-floor apartment, I was thinking that the man found my presence burdensome and that it was a mistake to visit him. But since in the end such considerations, as if on purpose, always drove me to creep further into an ambiguous position, I entered. It had been almost a year since I'd last seen Simonov.

III

I found two more of my schoolmates with him. They seemed to be discussing an important matter. They took scarcely any notice of my entrance, which was strange, since I hadn't seen them for years. Evidently they considered me something akin to a common fly. I hadn't been treated like that even at school, although everyone hated me there. I understood, of course, that they must despise me now because of my failure to make a career for myself in the civil service, and because I had sunk so low, went about badly dressed, and so on — which in their eyes was a sign of my lack of ability and my insignificance. Nevertheless, I hadn't expected such contempt. Simonov was positively surprised by my arrival. Even in the past he had always seemed surprised by my arrival. All this disconcerted me: I sat down, feeling rather miserable, and began listening to what they were saying.

They were engaged in a serious and even heated conversation about a farewell dinner they wanted to arrange jointly on the very next day for their schoolmate Zverkov, an army officer, who was departing for a distant province. M'sieur Zverkov had also been a schoolmate of mine all the while. I had begun to hate him particularly in the upper grades. In the lower grades he had simply been a pretty, playful boy whom everybody liked. I had hated him, however, even in the lower grades, precisely because he was a pretty and playful boy. He was always a poor student and got worse as he went on; he managed to graduate, however, because he had influential connections. During his last year at school he inherited an estate of two hundred serfs, and since almost all of us were poor, he'd even begun to brag. He was vulgar in the extreme, but at the same time he was a good-natured fellow, even when he was bragging. Despite superficial, fantastic, and highfalutin notions of honor and dignity, all but a very few of us positively groveled before Zverkov, and the more he bragged, the more his schoolmates groveled. And it wasn't to gain any profit or advantage that they groveled, but simply because he had been favored by the gifts of nature. Furthermore, Zverkov had somehow come to be regarded as an expert on tact and good manners. This last fact particularly infuriated me. I hated the abrupt, self-confident tone of his voice, his admiration of his own witticisms, which were often frightfully stupid, although he was bold in his language; I hated his handsome but stupid face (for which I would, however, have gladly traded my *intelligent* one), and his free-and-easy manners typical of officers in the "'forties."[15] I hated the way he talked about his future successes with women (he had made the decision not to get involved with women until he had his officer's epaulettes, and he was impatiently looking forward to them) and the way he boasted that he'd constantly be fighting duels. I remember how I, always so taciturn, suddenly tangled with Zverkov when, one day, during recess, talking with his schoolmates about his future exploits, about the "cherries" he would pluck, and growing as playful as a puppy in the sun, he suddenly announced that he wouldn't leave a single village maiden on his estate unnoticed, that that was his *droit de seigneur,* and that if the peasants dared protest, he would have them all flogged, the bearded bastards, and double the tax on them. Our louts applauded, but I decided to tangle with him, not out of any compassion for the maidens and their fathers, but simply because everyone was applauding such an insect. I got

15. That is, the 1840s. *Trans.*

the better of him that time, but Zverkov, though stupid, was cheerful and impudent, and so he laughed it off, and even in such a way that I didn't really get the better of him: he had the last laugh. Later he got the better of me on several occasions, without malice, but somehow jokingly, casually, laughingly. Spitefully and contemptuously, I refused to answer him. After graduation he tried to get together with me; I didn't resist too much, because it flattered me; but soon we quite naturally parted ways. Afterwards I heard about his barrack-room successes as a lieutenant, about his *carousing.* Then there were other rumors — of his *successes* in the service. By then he had stopped nodding to me in the street, and I suspected that he was afraid of compromising himself by acknowledging a person as insignificant as I was. I saw him once in the theater, in the third tier of boxes, already sporting an officer's gold braids. He was twisting and twirling about, ingratiating himself with the daughters of some ancient general. In three years he had let himself go considerably, although he was still rather handsome and agile; he'd begun to fill out, to gain a lot of weight; one could see that by the time he was thirty, he'd be quite corpulent. So it was for this Zverkov, who was getting ready to depart, that our schoolmates were planning to give a dinner. They had kept up with him these three years, although, inwardly, they didn't consider themselves on an equal footing with him — I'm convinced of that.

Of Simonov's two visitors, one was Ferfichkin, of Russified German stock, a little fellow with the face of a monkey, a fool who was always mocking everyone, a very bitter enemy of mine from our days in the lower grades — a vile, impudent, swaggering fellow who affected a most sensitive feeling of personal honor, although, of course, he was a wretched little coward at heart. He was one of those idolizers of Zverkov who groveled before him for his own ends, and often borrowed money from him. Simonov's other visitor, Trudoliubov, was a person in no way remarkable — a military man, tall, with a cold physiognomy, fairly honest, though he worshiped success of every sort and was capable of talking only about promotions. He was some sort of distant relation of Zverkov's, and this, foolish as it seems, gave him a certain importance among us. He always thought me as of no consequence whatever; but his behavior toward me, though not quite courteous, was tolerable.

"Well, with seven roubles each," said Trudoliubov, "that makes twenty-one roubles between the three of us — we can have a good dinner. Zverkov doesn't pay, of course."

"Of course not, since we're inviting him," Simonov agreed.

"Do you really think," Ferfichkin interrupted arrogantly and excitedly, like some insolent flunkey boasting of the decorations of his master the general, "do you really think Zverkov will let us pay for everything? He'll accept out of delicacy, but he'll order half a dozen bottles at his own expense."

"How can the four of us handle half a dozen?" observed Trudoliubov, taking notice only of the half dozen.

"So it's the three of us, with Zverkov for the fourth, twenty-one roubles, at the Hôtel de Paris, tomorrow at five o'clock," Simonov, who had been chosen to make the arrangements, concluded.

"What do you mean, twenty-one roubles?" I asked in some agitation, and even with a show of being offended. "If you count me, you'll have twenty-eight roubles, not twenty-one."

It seemed to me that to invite myself so suddenly and unexpectedly would be a beautiful gesture, and that they would all be conquered at once and would look at me with respect.

"Do you really want to come, too?" Simonov asked with displeasure, seeming to avoid looking at me. He knew me by heart.

It infuriated me that he knew me by heart.

"And why not? After all, I'm an old schoolmate of his, too, I believe; and I must confess that I even feel a bit offended that you've excluded me," I said, ready to boil over.

"And where were we to find you?" Ferfichkin rudely stuck himself into the conversation.

"You never were on good terms with Zverkov," Trudoliubov added, frowning. But I had already clutched at the idea and wouldn't let go of it.

"It seems to me that no one has a right to judge that," I objected with a tremor in my voice, as though God knows what had happened.

"Perhaps I want to come to the dinner now precisely because I haven't always been on good terms with him."

"Oh, who can understand you . . . always these elevated sublimities . . ." Trudoliubov said, laughing.

"We'll put your name down," Simonov decided, addressing me. "Tomorrow at five o'clock at the Hôtel de Paris. Make sure you get it right."

"What about the money?" Ferfichkin began in an undertone, nodding at me to Simonov, but he stopped, because even Simonov became embarrassed.

"That will do," said Trudoliubov, getting up. "If he wants to come so much, let him come."

"But we have our own circle, a circle of friends," Ferfichkin said angrily, as he, too, picked up his hat. "It's not an official gathering. Perhaps we don't want you at all. . . ."

They went away. Ferfichkin didn't nod to me at all as he departed, while Trudoliubov barely nodded without looking at me. Simonov, with whom I was left tête-à-tête, was in a state of irritated perplexity, and he looked at me strangely. He didn't sit down, nor did he invite me to sit down.

"Hmm . . . yes . . . tomorrow, then. Will you give me the money now? I just ask so as to know with certainty," he muttered in embarrassment.

I flushed with anger, but as I did so I remembered that from time immemorial I had owed Simonov fifteen roubles — which I had, indeed, never forgotten, although I had never repaid him, either.

"You'll understand, Simonov, that I couldn't have known when I came here . . . and I'm really annoyed with myself for forgetting. . . ."

"All right, all right — it doesn't matter. You can pay tomorrow at the dinner. I just wanted to know . . . Please don't . . ."

He broke off and began pacing the room in even greater irritation. As he paced, he began to plant his heels and to stomp more heavily.

"Am I keeping you?" I asked, after a two-minute silence.

"Oh, no!" he said, starting. "That is, actually — yes. You see, I have to drop in on someone . . . not far from here," he added in some sort of apologetic tone, somewhat embarrassed.

"My God, why didn't you say so?" I cried, grabbing my cap, though with an astonishingly free-and-easy air, which came from God knows where.

"It's really not far . . . only a few steps away," Simonov repeated, seeing me to the entryway with a fussy air which didn't suit him at all. "So, then, tomorrow at five sharp!" he shouted down the stairs after me. He was very glad I was leaving. But I was in a fury.

"What possessed me, what possessed me to force myself upon them?" I gnashed my teeth as I strode along the street. "And for a scoundrel, for a little pig like Zverkov! Of course I won't go; of course, I should just spit at them all. I'm not obligated in any way, am I? Tomorrow I'll send Simonov a note by the city post. . . ."

But what really made me furious was that I knew for certain that I'd go to the dinner, that I'd go on purpose; and the more tactless, the more unseemly it was for me to go, the more certain I'd be to go.

And there was even a positive obstacle to my going: I didn't have any money. All I had lying around was nine roubles. But of that I had to give seven tomorrow for monthly wages to my servant, Apollon, who lived with me for seven roubles, meals not included.

Not to pay him was impossible, considering Apollon's character. But I'll talk about that bastard, that festering sore of mine, some other time.

However, I knew that even so I wouldn't pay him, but would definitely go to the dinner.

That night I dreamt the most grotesque dreams. No wonder: all evening I had been oppressed by memories of my years of penal servitude at school, and I couldn't shake them off. I was shoved into that school by distant relations on whom I was dependent and about whom I've heard nothing since; I was shoved there, orphaned, already crushed by their reproaches, already pensive, taciturn, and gazing at everything with savage distrust. My schoolmates greeted me with malicious and merciless mockery because I wasn't like any of them. But I couldn't endure mockery; I couldn't get along with them as easily as they got along with one another. I hated them from the first, and shut myself away from everyone in a frightened, wounded, and inordinate pride. Their coarseness outraged me. They laughed cynically at my face, at my clumsy figure; and yet what stupid faces they had themselves! In our school the expressions of the boys' faces seemed to grow stupider and to degenerate in some special way. How many fine-looking boys came to us! In a few years they would become repulsive to look at. Even at sixteen I wondered at them morosely; even then I was astonished by the pettiness of their thoughts, the stupidity of their pursuits, their games, their conversations. They didn't understand the most essential things, they took no interest in the most striking, impressive subjects that I couldn't help considering them inferior to myself. It wasn't wounded vanity that drove me to this, and for God's sake don't come creeping at me with your hackneyed objection, repeated to the point of nausea, that I was only a dreamer, while even then they understood real life. They didn't understand anything; they had no idea of real life; and I swear that that's what outraged me most about them. On the contrary, they took the most obvious, striking reality in a fantastically stupid way, and even then were accustomed to worship only success. Everything that was just, but humiliated and looked down upon, they laughed at heartlessly and shamefully. They took rank for intelligence; even at sixteen they were already talking about snug positions. Of course, a great deal of this was due to their stupidity, to the bad examples with which they had constantly been surrounded in their childhood and boyhood. They were monstrously depraved. Of course, a great deal of that, too, was superficial, an air of cynicism they affected; of course, there were glimpses of youth and freshness even in their depravity; but even that freshness wasn't attractive, and showed itself in a kind of cockiness. I hated them terribly, although perhaps I was worse than any of them. They paid me back in kind, and didn't conceal their aversion for me. But by then I didn't desire their love; on the contrary, I constantly longed for their humiliation. To escape their mockery, I purposely began to make all the progress I could with my studies and broke through into the ranks of the best students. This impressed them. Furthermore, it gradually began to dawn on all of them that I had already read books none of them could read, and understood things (not forming part of our school curriculum) about which they had not even heard. They took a savage and mocking view of this, but they submitted morally, especially since even the teachers began to pay attention to me because of it. The mockery stopped, but the hostility remained, and cold, strained relations became permanent between us. In the end I wasn't able to endure it: as the years passed, a need for people, for friends, developed in me. I attempted to get close to some of my schoolmates, but these attempts always turned out to be unnatural and ended of their own accord. Once, indeed, I did have a friend. But I was already a tyrant at heart; I wanted to have unlimited power over his soul; I wanted to instill in him a contempt for his surroundings; I demanded of him a disdainful and complete break with those surroundings. I frightened him with my passionate friendship; I reduced him to tears, to hysterics; he was a naïve and giving soul; but when he gave himself to me entirely, I began to hate him immediately and pushed him away from me — as if all I needed him for was to win a victory over him, to subjugate him, and nothing else. But I couldn't defeat all of them; my friend wasn't at all like them either, but was in fact a very rare exception. The first thing I did on leaving school was to give up the special position for which I had been intended; I gave it up in order to break all ties, to curse the past and throw ashes on it. . . . And the devil only knows why, after all that, I should drag myself to see this Simonov!

The next morning I roused myself early and leaped out of bed in agitation, as if all of this were about to start happening right away. I believed that some radical break in my life was at hand, and that it would inevitably occur that day. It might have been out of lack of habit, but, all my life, any external event, however trivial, always made me feel as if some radical break in my life were at hand and about to occur immediately. Nevertheless, I went to the office as usual, but slipped away two hours early to go home and get ready. The main thing, I thought, is not to be the first to arrive, or they'll think I'm overjoyed at being invited. But there were thousands of such "main things" to consider, and they were all agitating me to the point where I became powerless. I polished my boots a second time with my own hands; nothing in the world would have induced Apollon to polish them twice a day, since he would have considered this to be against all laws. So I polished them myself, stealing the brushes from the entryway so that he wouldn't notice somehow and then despise me for it afterward. Then I meticulously examined my clothes and found that everything was old, worn, threadbare. I had let myself get too slovenly. My office uniform was perhaps in good condition, but I couldn't go to dinner in my office uniform. The worst thing was that, on my trousers, right on the knee, there was an enormous yellow stain. I had a foreboding that that stain alone would deprive me of nine-tenths of my personal dignity. I also knew that it was unseemly of me to think so. "But this isn't the time for thinking: reality is at hand," I thought, and my heart sank. I also knew perfectly well, even then, that I was monstrously exaggerating all these facts; but what could I do? I couldn't control myself; I was shaking with fever. In despair I pictured to myself how disdainfully and coldly that "scoundrel" Zverkov would greet me; with what dull-witted, invincible contempt the dullard Trudoliubov would look at me; how vilely and impudently that insect Ferfichkin would snigger at my expense, sucking up to Zverkov; how completely Simonov would understand all of it, and how he'd despise me for my wretched vanity and cowardice — and, worst of all, how paltry, *unliterary*, and commonplace it would all be. Of course, the best thing would be not to go at all. But that was the most impossible thing of all: whenever I feel impelled to do something, I plunge right in, head first. Then I'd have taunted myself for the rest of my life: "When it came to *reality*, you were a coward, a coward, a coward!" On the contrary, I passionately wanted to show all this "rabble" that I'm by no means the coward I'm making myself out to be. What's more, in the intensest paroxysm of this cowardly fever, I dreamt of gaining the upper hand, of defeating them, of carrying them away, of forcing them to love me — if only for "the sublimity of my thoughts and my indisputable wit." They'd abandon Zverkov; he'd sit in the corner, silent and embarrassed, and I'd crush him. Then, perhaps, I'd be reconciled with Zverkov, and we'd drink to our everlasting friendship; but what was most bitter and humiliating for me was that I knew even then, knew fully and for certain, that I didn't really need any of this, that I didn't really want to crush, subjugate, or attract them, and if I could have achieved all that, I'd be the first to say that it wasn't worth a penny. Oh, how I prayed to God that this day would pass quickly! In inexpressible anguish I kept going over to the window, opening the movable pane, and looking out into the troubled darkness of the thickly falling wet snow. . . .

Finally, my wretched little wall clock hissed out five. I grabbed my hat and, trying not to look at Apollon — who since morning had been waiting for me to pay him his wages but because of his pride was unwilling to be the first to speak about it — I slipped past him out the door and, in a coach I hired with my last half-rouble, I arrived like a lord at the Hôtel de Paris.

IV

I knew since the previous evening that I'd be the first one to arrive. But it was no longer a question of being first.

Not only was no one there, but I even had trouble finding our room. The table hadn't even been set. What did this mean? After a good many questions I finally elicited from the waiters that the dinner had been ordered not for five but for six o'clock. This was confirmed at the buffet too. I even felt ashamed to go on questioning them. It was only twenty-five minutes past five. If they had changed the dinner hour, they could at least have informed me — that's what the city post is for — and not subjected me to such "disgrace" both in my own eyes and . . . and in the waiters' eyes. I sat down; a waiter began to set the table; I felt even more humiliated when he was present. Towards six o'clock they brought in candles, which complemented the lamps that were already burning in the room. It hadn't occurred to the waiter, however, to bring them in at once when I arrived. In the next room, two gloomy, angry-looking customers were dining in silence at separate tables. There was a great deal of noise in a room further away; they were even shouting; one could hear the laughter of a crowd of people, and nasty little shrieks in French: there were ladies at the dinner. In short, it was extremely nauseating. Rarely had I passed a more unpleasant hour, so that when they did arrive all together precisely at six, I was overjoyed, at the first instant, to see them, as though they were my liberators, and nearly forgot that I was obliged to look offended.

Zverkov walked in at the head of them, obviously the leader. Both he and they were laughing; but, on seeing me, Zverkov assumed a dignified air, walked up to me unhurriedly, bending slightly at the waist, as if coquettishly, and offered me his hand in a friendly, but not overfriendly, fashion, with a sort of cautious courtesy like that of a general, as if in offering me his hand he was also guarding himself against something. I had imagined, on the contrary, that, as soon as he entered, he would break into his habitual thin, squealing laugh and start making his insipid jokes and witticisms. I had been getting ready for them since the previous evening, but I hadn't expected such condescension, such supercilious friendliness. So, he already entirely considered himself immeasurably superior to me in every respect? If he only meant to insult me by that supercilious general's attitude, it wouldn't have mattered, I thought; I'd be able to get back at him somehow. But what if, without the least desire to be insulting, the notion had crept into his dumb sheep's brain that he really was immeasurably superior to me and could only look at me in a patronizing way? The very supposition made me gasp for breath.

"I was surprised to hear of your desire to join us," he began, lisping and hissing, and elongating his words, something he hadn't done before. "You and I seem to have seen nothing of one another. You avoid us. You shouldn't. We're not as frightening as you might think. Well, sir, in any event, I'm gla-a-a-ad to rene-e-e-ew . . ."

And he turned casually to put his hat down on the windowsill.

"Have you been waiting long?" Trudoliubov asked.

"I arrived at five sharp, just as I was told to yesterday," I answered loudly and with an irritability that threatened an imminent explosion.

"Didn't you let him know that we changed the hour?" Trudoliubov asked Simonov.

"No, I didn't. I forgot," the latter replied, but without any sign of regret; and without even apologizing to me, he went off to order the hors d'oeuvres.

"So you've been here a whole hour? Oh, poor fellow!" Zverkov shouted sarcastically, because, according to his notions, this really was terribly funny. That villain Ferfichkin chimed in after him in his nasty, ringing little voice, yapping like a little mutt. In his eyes, too, my situation seemed very funny and embarrassing.

"It's not funny in the least!" I yelled at Ferfichkin, growing more and more irritated. "Other people are to blame, not me. They neglected to let me know. It's . . . it's . . . it's simply absurd."

"It's not only absurd, but something else as well," muttered Trudoliubov, naïvely taking my part. "You're being too polite. It was simply rudeness. Unintentional, of course. But how could Simonov . . . Hmm!"

"If a trick like that had been played on me," observed Ferfichkin, "I would . . ."

"But you should have ordered something for yourself," Zverkov interrupted, "or simply asked for dinner without waiting for us."

"You'll agree that I could have done that without asking anyone's permission," I snapped. "If I waited, it was because . . ."

"Let's sit down, gentlemen," cried Simonov, coming in. "Everything's ready; I can vouch for the champagne; it's chilled to perfection. . . . After all, I didn't know your address, so how could I find you?" He suddenly turned to me, but again he seemed to avoid looking at me. Evidently he had something against me. He had had time to think since yesterday.

They all sat down; I sat down, too. It was a round table. Trudoliubov was on my left, Simonov on my right. Zverkov was sitting opposite, Ferfichkin next to him, between him and Trudoliubov.

"S-o-o, you're . . . in the department?" Zverkov continued to occupy himself with me. Seeing that I was embarrassed, he imagined in earnest that he had to be nice to me and, so to speak, cheer me up. "Does he want me to throw a bottle at his head?" I thought, in a fury. Unaccustomed as I was to company, I was unnaturally quick to take offense.

"In the N — office," I answered curtly, looking at my plate.

"And . . . you f-f-find it prof-f-fitable? Tell me, what impe-e-lled you to leave your previous position?"

"What impe-e-e — ll-e-ed me was that I felt like leaving my previ-

67

ous position." My drawling was three times longer than his; I was now barely able to control myself. Ferfichkin guffawed. Simonov looked at me ironically; Trudoliubov stopped eating and began looking at me with curiosity.

Zverkov was jarred, but pretended not to notice.

"We-e-ell, what about your remu-u-u-neration?"

"What remu-u-u-u-neration are you talking about?"

"I mean, your s-s-salary."

"Are you cross-examining me?"

Nevertheless, I told him at once what my salary was. I turned terribly red.

"It's not very handsome," Zverkov observed majestically.

"No, sir, you can't afford to dine at cafe-restaurants on that!" Ferfichkin added insolently.

"To my thinking it's even paltry," Trudoliubov observed gravely.

"And how thin you've grown, how you've changed . . . since . . . ," added Zverkov, now not without a touch of venom in his voice, scrutinizing me and my attire with a sort of insolent compassion.

"Oh, don't embarrass him even more!" cried Ferfichkin, giggling.

"My dear sir, allow me to tell you that I am not embarrassed," I finally exploded. "Do you hear, sir? I'm dining here, in a 'cafe-restaurant,' at my own expense — at my own, not at other people's. Please take note of that, Monsieur Ferfichkin."

"Wha-a-at? Isn't everyone here dining at his own expense? You would seem to be . . ." Ferfitchkin lashed out at me, turning as red as a lobster, and looking me straight in the eye with fury.

"Ye-es," I answered, feeling I had gone too far, "and I imagine it would be better to talk of something more intelligent."

"You intend to show off your intelligence, I suppose?"

"Don't worry, that would be quite out of place here."

"What's all this cackling about, my dear sir? Have you lost your wits in that *duh*partment of yours?"

"Enough, gentlemen, enough!" Zverkov cried in a masterly way.

"How stupid this is!" muttered Simonov.

"It really is stupid. We've gathered here, a company of friends, to have a farewell dinner for our good friend, and you're settling old scores," Trudoliubov said, rudely addressing me alone. "You forced yourself upon us yesterday, so don't disrupt the general harmony. . . ."

"Enough, enough!" cried Zverkov. "Stop it, gentlemen, this won't do. Better let me tell you how I nearly got married two days ago. . . ."

And there followed a scandalous narrative about how this gentleman had nearly gotten married a few days before. There wasn't one word about the marriage, however, but the story was full of generals, colonels, and even court dignitaries, with Zverkov nearly playing the leading role among them. The story was greeted with approving laughter; Ferfichkin positively squealed.

No one paid any attention to me, and I sat crushed and humiliated.

"Lord in heaven, why am I associating with these people?" I thought. "And what a fool I've made of myself in front of them! I let Ferfichkin go too far, though. The numbskulls think they're doing me an honor by letting me sit down at their table; they don't understand that it's just the opposite: I'm doing them an honor! 'I've grown thinner! My clothes!' My damn trousers! Zverkov immediately noticed the yellow stain on my knee. . . . But what's the use! I should get up right away, this very minute, take my hat, and just leave, without saying a word. . . . Out of contempt! And tomorrow, a duel. The scoundrels! As though I cared about the seven roubles. They may think . . . To hell with it! I don't care about the seven roubles. I'm leaving this very minute!"

It goes without saying that I stayed.

In my misery I drank Lafite and sherry by the glassful. Because I was unaccustomed to it, I rapidly started to get drunk, and my annoyance grew as I got drunker. I suddenly had the desire to insult all of them in the most brazen manner and only then leave. To seize the moment and show my strength. Let them say, He may be ridiculous, but he's intelligent . . . and . . . and . . . in short, to hell with them all!

I surveyed all of them insolently with bleary eyes. But it was as if they had completely forgotten about me. They were noisy, they were shouting, they were cheerful. Zverkov kept on talking. I began to listen. Zverkov was telling about some majestic lady from whom he had finally succeeded in eliciting a confession of love (of course, he was lying through his teeth), and about how he had been specially helped in this business by an intimate friend of his, a certain princeling, the hussar Kolya, who had three thousand serfs.

"And yet this Kolya, who has three thousand serfs, hasn't even come to see you off." I suddenly intruded myself into the conversation. For a moment everyone was silent.

"You're drunk already," Trudoliubov said, finally deigning to notice me and glancing contemptuously in my direction. Zverkov was silently examining me as if I were an insect. I lowered my eyes. Simonov hurriedly began pouring champagne.

Trudoliubov lifted his glass; everyone did the same, except for me.

"To your health and to good luck on the journey!" he shouted to Zverkov. "To old times, gentlemen, and to our future! Hurrah!"

They all drank, and crowded round Zverkov to kiss him. I didn't move; my full glass stood untouched before me.

"Aren't you going to drink it?" roared Trudoliubov, losing his patience and turning threateningly toward me.

"I want to make a speech separately, on my own account . . . and then I'll drink it, Monsieur Trudoliubov."

"Spiteful brute!" muttered Simonov.

I drew myself up in my chair and feverishly took up my glass, preparing myself for something extraordinary, although I didn't know precisely what I was going to say.

"*Silence!*"[16] cried Ferfichkin. "Now for a display of wit!" Zverkov waited very gravely, knowing what was coming.

"Monsieur Lieutenant Zverkov," I began, "let me tell you that I hate phrases, phrase-mongers, and corseted waists. . . . That's the first point, and there's a second one to follow."

There was a general stir.

"The second point: I hate cherry-picking and cherry-pickers. Especially cherry-pickers!"[17]

16. In the original this word is in French. *Trans.*

17. In Russian these are *klubnichka* and *klubnichniki*, literally "strawberry-picking" and "strawberry-pickers." "Strawberry-picking" is how Nozdryov in Gogol's *Dead Souls* refers to erotic escapades. *Trans.*

"The third point: I love justice, truthfulness, and honesty." I continued almost mechanically, because I was beginning to grow ice-cold with horror, not understanding how I could be saying all this. "I love thought, M'sieur Zverkov; I love true comradeship, on an equal footing and not . . . hmm . . . I love . . . But, after all, why not? I, too, will drink to your health, M'sieur Zverkov. Seduce the Circassian maidens, shoot the enemies of the fatherland, and . . . and . . . To your health, M'sieur Zverkov!"

Zverkov got up from his chair, bowed to me, and said:

"I'm very grateful to you."

He was terribly offended and even turned pale.

"What the hell is going on?" roared Trudoliubov, slamming his fist down on the table.

"Well, sir, people are punched in the face for something like that!" squealed Ferfichkin.

"We should kick him out!" growled Simonov.

"Not a word, gentlemen, not a movement!" Zverkov exclaimed solemnly, putting a stop to the general indignation. "I'm grateful to all of you, but I can show him myself how much value I attach to his words."

"Monsieur Ferfichkin, tomorrow you'll give me satisfaction for the words you've just uttered!" I said loudly, addressing Ferfichkin with dignity.

"A duel, you mean? Certainly, sir," he answered. But I must have been so ridiculous when I challenged him, and it must have seemed so out of keeping with my entire appearance, that everyone, including Ferfichkin, nearly fell down with laughter.

"Better to let him alone! He's completely drunk," Trudoliubov said with disgust.

"I'll never forgive myself for letting him join us!" Simonov growled again.

"Now's the time to throw a bottle at their heads," I thought to myself as I picked up the bottle . . . and filled my glass.

"No, I'd better sit it out to the very end!" I kept thinking. "You'd be delighted, gentlemen, if I left. But nothing doing! I'll purposely go on sitting here and drinking to the very end, as a sign that I don't think you of the slightest consequence. I'll go on sitting and drinking, because this is a tavern and I paid good money to get in. I'll go on sitting and drinking, because I consider you to be so many pawns, so many nonexistent pawns. I'll go on sitting and drinking . . . and singing if I want to, yes, sir, singing, because I have the right to . . . to sing . . . hmm!"

But I didn't sing. I just tried not to look at any of them: I assumed the most carefree poses and waited impatiently for them to speak to me *first.* But alas, they didn't speak to me! And oh, how I wished, how I wished at that moment to be reconciled with them! The clock struck eight, and finally nine. They moved from the table to the sofa. Zverkov stretched himself on the couch, resting one foot on a little round table. The wine was also brought there. He did, as a matter of fact, order three bottles at his own expense. Naturally, he didn't invite me. They all sat round him on the sofa. They listened to him almost with reverence. It was evident that they loved him. "But why? Why?" I wondered. From time to time a drunken rapture would possess them, and they'd exchange kisses. They talked about the Caucasus, about the nature of true passion, about galbik,[18] about profitable positions in the service, about the income of a hussar called Podkharzhevsky, whom none of them knew personally, and rejoiced that he had a large income; about the extraordinary beauty and grace of a Princess D., whom none of them had ever seen; and finally it came to Shakespeare's being immortal.

I was smiling contemptuously and pacing up and down the other side of the room, opposite the sofa, along the wall, from the table to the stove and back again. I tried my very utmost to show them that I could do without them, and yet I purposely banged the floor with my boots, stomping it with my heels. But it was all for nothing: *they* didn't pay any attention. I had the patience to pace up and down in front of them from eight o'clock till eleven, in the same place, from the table to the stove and back again from the stove to the table. "I'm pacing up and down to please myself and no one can stop me." A waiter who kept coming into the room paused several times to look at me: My head was spinning from the frequent turns; there were moments when it seemed to me that I was de-

18. Galbik is a card game. *Trans.*

lirious. In the course of those three hours, I was drenched with sweat three times and became dry again. At times, a certain thought would pierce my heart with the deepest, most poisonous pain: that ten years, twenty years, forty years would pass, and that even after forty years I would still remember with loathing and humiliation these filthiest, most ludicrous, and most horrible moments of my entire life. It was impossible to humiliate oneself more shamelessly and more willingly, and I understood this completely, completely, but nevertheless I kept pacing up and down from the table to the stove and back again. "Oh, if you only knew what feelings and thoughts I'm capable of, and how cultured I am!" I thought at times, mentally addressing the sofa where my enemies were sitting. But my enemies behaved as if I weren't even in the room. Once, and only once, they turned towards me, precisely when Zverkov started talking about Shakespeare, and I suddenly burst into contemptuous laughter. I laughed in such an affected and vile way that they all immediately broke off their conversation and observed me in silence for about two minutes, seriously, without laughing, as I paced up and down along the wall from the table to the stove and *paid not the slightest attention to them*. But nothing came of it; they didn't speak to me, and two minutes later they ceased to notice me again. The clock struck eleven.

"Gentlemen," cried Zverkov, rising from the couch. "It's time for us to make our way *there!*"

"Of course, of course," the others assented.

I turned sharply toward Zverkov. I was so tormented, so broken, that I would have cut my throat to put an end to it. I was in a fever; my hair, soaked with sweat, stuck to my forehead and temples.

"Zverkov, I ask your forgiveness," I said abruptly and decisively. "Ferfichkin, yours too, and everyone's, everyone's. I've insulted you all!"

"Aha! So, a duel isn't in your line!" Ferfichkin hissed venomously.

A knife had been stuck into my heart.

"No, it's not the duel I'm afraid of, Ferfichkin! I'm ready to fight you tomorrow, but only after our reconciliation. I insist upon it, in fact, and you can't refuse. I want to prove to you that I'm not afraid of a duel. You'll fire first, and I'll fire into the air."

"He's indulging himself," Simonov remarked.

"He's simply raving!" Trudoliubov commented.

"But let us pass. Why are you standing in our way? What is it you want?" Zverkov asked contemptuously. They were all flushed; their eyes were glazed; they had been drinking heavily.

"I ask for your friendship, Zverkov. I insulted you, but . . ."

"Insulted? Y-y-you? Insulted m-m-me? Understand, sir, that you never, under any circumstances, could possibly insult *me*."

"And that's enough out of you. Get out of the way!" Trudoliubov concluded. "We're going."

"Olympia is mine, gentlemen — that's agreed!" shouted Zverkov.

"Agreed! Agreed!" the others answered, laughing.

I stood as though spat upon. The party was noisily leaving the room. Trudoliubov starting singing some stupid song. Simonov remained behind for a fraction of a moment to tip the waiters. I suddenly went up to him.

"Simonov! Give me six roubles!" I said decisively and desperately.

He looked at me in extreme amazement, with vacant eyes. He, too, was drunk.

"You don't mean you're going *there* with us?"

"Yes!"

"I don't have any money," he snapped, laughed contemptuously, and headed out of the room.

I grabbed hold of his overcoat. It was a nightmare.

"Simonov! I saw you had money. Why do you refuse me? Am I a scoundrel? Beware of refusing me: if you knew, if you only knew why I'm asking! Everything depends on it — my whole future, all my plans . . ."

Simonov pulled out the money and almost flung it at me.

"Take it, if you're so shameless!" he pronounced pitilessly, and ran to overtake the others.

For a moment I was left alone. Disorder, the remains of dinner, a broken glass on the floor, spilled wine, cigarette butts, drunkenness and delirium in my head, an agonizing misery in my heart, and finally the waiter, who had seen everything and heard everything and was looking inquisitively into my eyes.

"*There!* I'm going *there!*" I cried. "Either they'll all fall down on their knees to embrace my feet and beg for my friendship, or . . . I'll give Zverkov a slap in the face!"

V

"So this is it, this is it at last: a collision with reality," I muttered as I ran headlong down the stairs. "This is a far cry from the pope's leaving Rome and going to Brazil; it's a far cry from the ball on the shores of Lake Como!"

"You're a scoundrel," it flashed through my mind, "if you can laugh at that now."

"I don't care!" I cried, answering myself. "All is lost now anyway!"

There was no trace of them, but it didn't matter. I knew where they were going.

At the entrance stood a solitary late-night cabby in a coarse peasant coat, all dusted with the wet and seemingly warm snow that was still falling. It was steamy and stuffy. His shaggy little piebald horse was also dusted with snow, and it was coughing; I remember that very well. I made a rush for the roughly made sledge; but as soon as I raised my foot to get into it, the recollection of how Simonov had just given me six roubles took my legs out from under me, and I tumbled into the sledge like a sack.

"No, a great deal needs to be done to redeem all this!" I cried. "But I will redeem it or perish on the spot this very night. Let's go!"

We drove off. There was a veritable whirlwind spinning in my head.

"They won't fall down on their knees to beg for my friendship. That's a mirage, a vulgar mirage, revolting, romantic, and fantastic — the same thing as a ball on the shores of Lake Como. Therefore, I *must* give Zverkov a slap in the face! It's my duty. And so it's settled; I'm rushing there now to give him a slap in the face."

"Faster!"

The driver tugged at the reins.

"I'll slap him as soon as I go in. Before slapping him, should I say a few words by way of preface? No! I'll simply go in and slap him. They'll all be sitting in the drawing room, and he'll be sitting on the sofa with Olympia. That damned Olympia! She once laughed at my face and refused me. I'll pull Olympia by the hair, and Zverkov by the ears! No, better if I pull him by one ear, and drag him around the room. Maybe they'll all begin beating me and kick me out. That's probably what will happen. It doesn't matter! Anyway, I'll slap him first; it'll be my initiative; and according to the code of honor, that's the only thing that matters. He'll be branded and won't be able to wipe the slap off with any blows. Only a duel can wipe it off. He'll have to fight. And let them give me a beating now. Let them, the ungrateful wretches! Trudoliubov will beat me the hardest, because he's so strong; Ferfichkin will be sure to catch hold sideways and will undoubtedly tug at my hair. But it doesn't matter! That's why I'm going there. The blockheads will finally be forced to see the tragedy of it all! When they're dragging me to the door, I'll call out to them that in reality they're not worth my little finger."

"Faster, driver, faster!" I shouted to the cabby. He even jumped and cracked his whip, so savage was my shout.

"We'll fight at dawn — that's settled. I'm through with the department. Ferfichkin made a joke about it, calling it my *duh*partment. But where do I get the pistols? Nonsense! I'll get my salary in advance and buy them. And what about the gunpowder, and the bullets? That's the second's business. And how can all this be done by dawn? And where am I going to get a second? I don't have any friends."

"Nonsense!" I shouted, whipping myself up into even more of a frenzy. "Nonsense! The first person I meet on the street is obliged to be my second, just as he'd be obliged to pull a drowning man out of the water. The most eccentric cases must be allowed for. Even if I were to ask the director himself to be my second tomorrow, he'd have to consent, if only out of a sense of chivalry, and he'd have to keep it a secret! Anton Antonych . . ."

The fact is that at that moment I was more clearly and vividly aware than anyone else in the world of the whole loathsome absurdity of my plans and of the whole other side of the coin, but . . .

"Faster, driver, faster, you villain!"

"Please don't shout, sir!" this son of the earth replied.

A chill suddenly came over me.

"Wouldn't it be better . . . wouldn't it be better . . . to go straight home now? My God! Why, why did I invite myself to that dinner yesterday? But no, it's impossible. And my strolling up and down for three hours from the table to the stove? No, they, they and no one else must pay me for that stroll! They must wash away that dishonor!"

"Faster!"

"But what if they have me arrested? They wouldn't dare! They'd be afraid of the scandal. And what if Zverkov is so contemptuous that he refuses to fight a duel? That's even likely, but in that case I'll show them. . . . I'll rush to the post station when he's setting off tomorrow, I'll grab him by the leg, and I'll tear off his overcoat when he's getting into the carriage. I'll sink my teeth into his hand; I'll bite him. 'See what lengths you can drive a desperate man to!' It's all right if he hits me on the head and all of them beat me from behind. I'll shout to the assembled multitude, 'Look at this young puppy who's going off to seduce the Circassian maidens with my spittle on his face!'

"Of course, after that, everything will be over! The department will have disappeared from the face of the earth. I'll be arrested, I'll be tried, I'll be dismissed from the service, I'll be thrown into prison, and I'll be sent to Siberia, exiled.[19] It doesn't matter! Fifteen years later when they release me from prison, I'll drag myself after him, in rags, a beggar. I'll find him in some provincial town. He'll be married and happy. He'll have a grown daughter. . . . I'll say to him, 'Look, you monster, look at my hollow cheeks and my rags! I've lost everything — my career, my happiness, art, science, *the woman I loved* — and all because of you. I've brought pistols. I've come to discharge my pistol, and . . . and I . . . forgive you.' Then I'll fire into the air, and nothing more will be heard of me — not the faintest of echoes. . . ."

I was on the point of tears, although I knew perfectly well at that

19. Dostoevsky himself was imprisoned and exiled after his arrest for revolutionary activity. *Trans.*

instant that all this was out of Silvio and Lermontov's *Masquerade*.[20] And all at once I felt terribly ashamed, so ashamed that I stopped the horse, climbed out of the sledge, and stood there in the snow in the middle of the street. The driver stared at me in astonishment and sighed.

What was I to do? I couldn't go there — that was stupid. But I couldn't leave things as they were, either, because that would seem as though . . . Lord God! But how could I leave things as they were! After such insults!

"No!" I cried, throwing myself into the sledge again. "It's preordained! It's fate! Drive on, drive on! I'm going there!"

And in my impatience I punched the driver in the neck.

"What's the matter with you? Why are you hitting me?" the little peasant cried, whipping the nag, however, so that she began to kick up her hind legs.

The wet snow was falling in thick flakes; I uncovered myself, not caring about the snow. I forgot about everything else, because I had finally made up my mind to slap him, and felt with horror that it would *inevitably* happen now, at once, and that *no power could stop it now*. The deserted streetlamps gleamed morosely in the snowy darkness like torches at a funeral. The snow got under my overcoat, under my jacket, under my necktie, and melted there; I didn't cover myself; everything was lost, anyway! Finally, we drove up. I jumped out, almost senseless, ran up the steps, and began knocking and kicking at the door. I felt terribly weak, particularly in my legs and knees. They opened the door quickly, as if they knew I was coming. (As a matter of fact, Simonov had warned them that there might be one more, and this was a place where one had to give warning and generally to take precautions. This was one of those "fashionable shops" of the period which have long since been eradicated by the police. By day it really was a shop, but in the evenings, if one had an introduction, one might visit it for other purposes.)

---

20. Silvio, the protagonist of Pushkin's story "The Shot" (1830), dedicated his entire life to revenge. A similar role is played by the character Incognitio in Lermontov's drama *Masquerade* (1835). *Trans.*

I passed with quick steps through the dark shop into the familiar drawing room, where there was only one little candle burning, and stopped in perplexity: there was no one there.

"Where are they?" I asked somebody.

But by now, of course, they had managed to disperse. . . .

Before me stood a person with a stupid smile, the madam herself, who knew me slightly. A minute later the door opened, and another person came in.

Taking no notice of anything, I was striding about the room and, I think, talking to myself. It was as though I had been rescued from death, and I felt this joyously with my whole being: after all, I would have given the slap, I would certainly, certainly have given the slap! But now they weren't here and . . . everything had disappeared, everything had changed! I looked around. I wasn't yet able to take stock of what had happened. I looked mechanically at the girl who had entered: before me I glimpsed a fresh, young, rather pale face with straight, dark eyebrows, and with a serious, as if somewhat astonished, expression on her face. I liked this at once; I would have hated her if she'd been smiling. I began looking at her more intently and as if with effort: I hadn't fully collected my thoughts. There was something simple and good-natured in her face, but also something strangely serious. I'm certain this stood in her way here, and that those fools hadn't noticed her. One could not, however, call her a beauty, although she was tall, strong, well-built. Her clothing was extremely simple. Something foul bit me; I went straight up to her. . . .

By chance I looked in a mirror. My agitated face struck me as revolting in the extreme: pale, evil, vile, with disheveled hair. "It doesn't matter; I'm glad of it," I thought. "I'm even glad that I'll appear revolting to her; that gives me pleasure. . . ."

VI

Somewhere behind a partition, a clock began wheezing, as if from some strong pressure, as if someone were strangling it. After an unnaturally prolonged wheezing, there followed a shrill, nasty, and somehow unexpectedly frequent chiming — as if someone had suddenly jumped forward. It struck two. I came to my senses, although I hadn't been asleep, but had only been lying there in a semi-stupor.

It was almost completely dark in the narrow, cramped, low-ceilinged room, which was encumbered with an enormous wardrobe and cluttered with cartons, rags, and all sorts of old clothes. The candle end that had been burning on the table at the other end of the room was going out and flickered faintly from time to time. In a few minutes total darkness would engulf the room.

It didn't take me long to come out of my stupor; I remembered everything at once, without any effort, as though it had been lying in ambush to pounce on me again. And even when I was in my stupor, it was as if some sort of point constantly remained in my memory which I couldn't forget and around which my delirious dreams moved heavily. But, strange to say, everything that had happened to me that day seemed to me now, upon awakening, to have happened in the deeply remote past, as if it had been another life.

I was in a daze. Something seemed to be flying back and forth above me, and brushing against me, exciting me, agitating me. Misery and spite were surging up in me again and seeking an outlet. Suddenly, right beside me, I saw two wide-open eyes examining me curiously and persistently. The look in those eyes was coldly indifferent, sullen, as if utterly alien; it oppressed me.

A grim idea was born in my brain and passed through my entire body like some sort of nasty sensation, like the one you get when you enter some damp and moldy underground. It was somehow unnatural that those two eyes had only now decided to begin examining me. I also remembered that in the course of two hours I hadn't said a single word to this creature and had considered it quite unnecessary to do so; that had even pleased me for some reason. But now, all of a sudden, there vividly came to me the absurd idea — repulsive as a spider — of debauchery, which, without love, grossly and shamelessly begins precisely where true love finds its consummation. We looked at each other like that for a long time, but she didn't lower her eyes before mine, and her expression didn't change, so that, in the end, for some reason, this made me weirdly uneasy.

"What's your name?" I asked abruptly, to put an end to it quickly.

"Liza," she answered, almost in a whisper, but somehow far from graciously, and she turned her eyes away.

I was silent.

"The weather today . . . the snow . . . it's nasty!" I muttered, almost to myself, putting my arm under my head despondently and looking at the ceiling.

She didn't answer. The whole thing was grotesque.

"Are you from around here?" I asked a minute later, almost angrily, turning my head slightly towards her.

"No."

"Where are you from?"

"From Riga," she muttered reluctantly.

"Are you German?"

"No, Russian."

"Have you been here long?"

"Where?"

"In this house?"

"Two weeks." She spoke more and more curtly. The candle went out; I could no longer distinguish her face.

"Are your father and mother still living?"

"Yes . . . no . . . yes, they're still living."

"Where are they?"

"There . . . in Riga."

"Who are they?"

"Just . . ."

"Just what? What class are they?"

"Tradespeople."

"Have you always lived with them?"

"Yes."

"How old are you?"

"Twenty."

"Why did you leave them?"

"Oh, for no reason."

That "For no reason" meant "Kiss off — this nauseates me." We were silent.

Only God knows why I didn't leave. I myself felt more and more nauseated and depressed. Confused images of the entire previous day began to pass through my memory, somehow all on their own, without my willing it. I suddenly remembered a scene that I'd witnessed on the street that morning when, full of cares, I was hurrying to the office.

"They were carrying a coffin out today and nearly dropped it," I suddenly said aloud, not with the desire to begin a conversation but almost by accident.

"A coffin?"

"Yes, in the Haymarket; they were carrying it out of a cellar."

"Out of a cellar?"

"Not out of a cellar exactly, but out of a basement . . . oh, you know . . . from down below . . . out of a house of ill repute. It was filthy all around. . . . Eggshells, litter . . . a stench. It was vile."

Silence.

"A nasty day to be buried!" I began again, just to break the silence.

"Why nasty?"

"Snow, slush . . ." (I yawned.)

"It makes no difference," she said suddenly, after a brief silence.

"No, it's vile . . ." (I yawned again.) "The gravediggers must have cursed because the snow was drenching them. And there must have been water in the grave."

"Why was there water in the grave?" she asked, with a certain curiosity, but she spoke even more rudely and curtly than before. Something suddenly began to provoke me.

"Why, there must have been water at the bottom half a foot deep. You can't dig a dry grave in Volkovo Cemetery."

"Why not?"

"What do you mean, why not? The place is waterlogged. There are swamps everywhere. So they put them in the water. I've seen it myself . . . many times."

(I'd never seen it once, and in fact I'd never even been to Volkovo, but had only heard stories of it.)

"Doesn't it matter to you how you die?"

"But why should I die?" she answered, as though defending herself.

"Why, someday you'll die, and you'll die exactly like that woman this morning. She was . . . a girl like you. She died of consumption."

"A working girl would have died in the hospital. . . ." (She knows all about it already, I thought: she said "working girl," not just "girl.")

"She owed money to her madam," I retorted, more and more provoked by the argument, "and continued working for her almost up to the end, even though she had consumption. The cabbies were standing around and talking to some soldiers, telling them all about it. No doubt they were her acquaintances. They were laughing. They were planning to drink to her memory in a tavern." (I had fabricated much of this.)

Silence followed, deep silence. She didn't even stir.

"So, it's better to die in the hospital, is it?"

"Isn't it just the same? Besides, why should I die?" she added irritably.

"If not now, then later?"

"Well, then later . . ."

"That's what you think! Now you're young, pretty, fresh — you fetch a high price. But after a year of this life, you won't be the same — you'll fade."

"After a year?"

"In any case, after a year you'll be worth less," I continued sadistically. "You'll go from here to some place lower, to some other house. A year later, to a third house — lower and lower, and in seven years or so you'll end up in a basement on the Haymarket. That is, if you're lucky. But it would be much worse if you contracted some sickness, consumption, say . . . or caught a chill, or something or other. It's not easy to get over a sickness in your way of life. It'll latch onto you and won't let go. And so you'll die."

"Oh, well, then I'll die," she answered, quite angrily, and she made a quick movement.

"But one is sorry."

"Sorry for whom?"

83

"Sorry for life."

Silence.

"You had a fiancé, didn't you?"

"What's that to you?"

"Oh, I'm not cross-examining you. It's nothing to me. Why are you so angry? Of course, you may have had your own troubles. What is it to me? It's simply that I felt sorry."

"Sorry for whom?"

"Sorry for you."

"No need to be," she whispered, barely audibly, and again made a movement.

That incensed me at once. What! I was so gentle with her, and she . . .

"So, you think you're on the right path? Is that it?"

"I don't think anything."

"That's what's wrong, that you don't think. Come to your senses while there's still time. And there still is time. You're still young, pretty; you could fall in love, get married, be happy. . . ."

"Not all married women are happy," she snapped in her former rude, curt manner.

"Not all of them, of course, but it's still much better than the life here. Incomparably better. Besides, with love one can live even without happiness. Life is good even in sorrow; it's good to live in the world, no matter how you live. But here, what do you have except . . . foulness? Phew!"

I turned away in disgust; I was no longer reasoning coldly. I began to feel what I was saying, and grew excited. I was longing to expound my cherished *little ideas* which I had hatched in my corner. Something suddenly flared up in me; some sort of goal "appeared" before me.

"Don't pay attention to the fact that I'm here; I'm no model for you. I may even be worse than you are. Anyway, I was drunk when I came here," I hastened, nonetheless, to justify myself. "Besides, a man's no model for a woman. It's a different thing; I may degrade and defile myself, but I'm nobody's slave; if I want to leave, I just get up and go. I shake it off, and I'm a new man. But you're a slave from the start. Yes, a slave! You give up everything, all your freedom. And if you want to break your chains afterwards, you won't be able to; they'll bind you more and more tightly. It's such an accursed chain. I know it. I won't even talk about the other things; you might not even understand; but tell me this: no doubt you already owe money to the madam? There, you see!" I added, even though she hadn't answered, but only listened silently, with her whole being. "That's a chain for you! You'll never buy your freedom. They'll see to that. It's like selling your soul to the devil. . . . And besides . . . how do you know — maybe I'm just as unfortunate as you are, and I'm wallowing in the filth on purpose, out of misery? After all, men take to drink out of grief; well, I'm here out of grief. Now, tell me, where's the good in any of this? Here you and I . . . came together . . . a while ago, and all that time we didn't say one word to each other, and only afterwards you began staring at me like a wild creature, and I did the same. Is that how people love one another? Is that how one human being is supposed to encounter another? It's grotesque — that's what it is!"

"Yes!" she agreed, abruptly and quickly. I was even surprised by how quickly she uttered this "yes." So the same thought may have been roaming in her head when she was examining me earlier. So she, too, was capable of certain thoughts? "Damn it all, this is curious — there's a *kinship* between us!" I thought, almost rubbing my hands with delight. "And, indeed, how can I fail to get the better of such a young soul?"

It was the game that attracted me most.

She turned her head closer to me, and it appeared to me in the darkness that she propped herself up on her arm. Perhaps she was examining me. How sorry I was that I couldn't see her eyes. I heard her deep breathing.

"Why did you come to this house?" I began, now with a sense of power.

"Just because . . ."

"But how nice it is to live in your father's house! You're warm, you're free; you have your own nest."

"But what if it's worse than that?"

"I must take the right tone," it flashed through my mind. "I may not get far with sentimentality."

However, that merely flashed through my mind. I swear, she really did interest me. Besides, I was somewhat exhausted and susceptible to emotion. And, after all, cunning so easily goes hand-in-hand with feeling.

"Who denies it?" I hastened to answer. "Anything can happen. I'm convinced that someone has wronged you, and that you're more sinned against than sinning. Of course, I know nothing of your story, but it's not likely a girl like you has ended up here of her own inclination. . . ."

"A girl like me? What kind of girl am I?" she whispered, barely audibly; but I heard it.

Damn it all, I was flattering her. That's vile. But perhaps it was a good thing. . . . She was silent.

"You see, Liza — I'll tell you about myself! If I'd had a family when I was growing up, I wouldn't be what I am now. I often think about this. However bad it may be in a family, they're still your father and mother — they're not enemies or strangers. Once a year at least, they'll show their love for you. At least you know you're in your own home. . . . I grew up without a family, and that's probably why I've turned out so . . . unfeeling."

I bided my time again.

"Maybe she doesn't understand," I thought. "And it really is ridiculous — this moralizing."

"If I were a father and had a daughter, I think I would love my daughter more than my sons, really," I began indirectly, as if talking about something else, in order to distract her attention. I confess I was blushing.

"Why is that so?" she asked.

Ah! So she was listening!

"I just would. I really don't know, Liza. You see, I knew a father who was a stern, severe man, but he used to go down on his knees before his daughter; he used to kiss her hands, her feet; he couldn't admire her enough, really. When she danced at parties, he used to stand in one spot for five hours at a stretch, not taking his eyes off her. He was crazy about her; I can understand that! At night she'd get tired and fall asleep, and he'd wake up and go kiss her and make the sign of the cross over her while she slept. He himself would go about in a dirty old jacket; he was stingy with everyone else, but he would spend his last penny on her, giving her expensive presents, and it was his greatest joy if she was pleased with his present. Fathers always love their daughters more than the mothers do. Some girls live happily at home! And I believe I would never let my daughter marry."

"Why not?" she said, with a faint smile.

"I'd be jealous, honest to God. To think that she should kiss anyone else! That she should love a stranger more than her father! It's painful to imagine. Of course, that's all nonsense; of course, every father would be reasonable in the end. But I believe that before I gave her in marriage, I'd worry myself to death: I'd find fault with all her suitors. But in the end I'd give her to the one she herself loved. After all, the one whom the daughter loves always seems the worst to the father. That's how it is. So many family troubles come from that."

"Some are glad to sell their daughters, instead of giving them honorably in marriage," she muttered suddenly.

Ah, so that was it!

"Such a thing happens, Liza, in those accursed families in which there's neither God nor love," I retorted with passion. "And where there's no love, there's no sense, either. There are such families, it's true, but I'm not speaking of them. Obviously, you didn't see much kindness in your own family, if you talk like that. You must be genuinely unfortunate. Hmm. . . . That sort of thing mostly happens because of poverty."

"And is it any better with the gentry? Honest people live decently even in poverty."

"Hmm . . . yes. Perhaps. Another thing, Liza: Man likes to count his misery, but he doesn't count his happiness. But if he were to count properly, he'd see that everyone gets his share of happiness. Well, and what if everything goes well in the family, God blesses it, your husband turns out to be a good man, he loves you, cherishes you, never leaves you? It's good to be in such a family! Sometimes it's good even when

87

there's misery; and where isn't there misery? Perhaps, if you marry, *you'll find out for yourself.* Consider even the first years of married life with the one you love: what happiness, what happiness there sometimes is in it! I mean, all the time. In those early days, even quarrels with one's husband end happily. With some women, the more they love their husbands, the more they like to start quarrels with them. Indeed, I knew a woman like that; it was as if she was saying, 'My love for you is powerful, and I'm tormenting you because of my love, so that you should feel it.' Do you know it's possible to torment a person on purpose out of love? Women especially like to do that. They think to themselves, 'Afterwards I'll love him so, I'll caress him so, that it's no sin to torment him a little now.' And at home everyone rejoices looking at you, and things are good and merry and peaceful and honorable. . . . Then there are women who are jealous. I knew a woman who, if her husband went off anywhere, couldn't restrain herself, but would rush out at night to inquire on the sly, 'Is he there, is he in that house, is he with that woman?' Now that's wrong. And she knows it's wrong, and her heart fails her and torments itself, but, after all, she loves him: it's all because of love. And how good it is to make up after quarrels, to admit her guilt before him or to forgive him! And it's so good for both of them, it suddenly becomes so good — as if they've met anew, been married anew, as if their love has begun anew. And no one, no one should know what passes between husband and wife if they love each another. And whatever quarrels there may be between them, no one, not even a mother, should be called in to judge between them and hear them tell about each other. They are their own judges. Love is a divine mystery and should be hidden from the eyes of strangers, no matter what happens. That makes it holier and better. They respect each other more, and much is based on respect. And if once there has been love, if they married for love, why should love vanish? Surely one can sustain it! It's rare that one cannot sustain it. And if the husband turns out to be kind and honest, why shouldn't love last? The early conjugal love will pass, it's true, but then there'll come a love that is even better. There'll be a union of souls; they'll have everything in common; there'll be no secrets between them. And they'll have children, and here the most difficult times

88

will seem happy to them, as long as they love and have courage. Even work will be joyful; at times you will deny yourself bread for the sake of your children, and even that will be joyful. They'll love you for it afterwards, so you're saving for your own future. As the children are growing up, you feel that you're an example for them, that you're a support for them; that even after you die, they'll keep your thoughts and feelings inside themselves all their lives, because they've received them from you; they'll take on your image and likeness. So, you see, this is a great duty. How can it fail to draw the father and mother closer together? They say it's a trial to have children. Who says that? It's a heavenly happiness! Do you love little children, Liza? I love them terribly. You know: a little rosy baby boy is sucking at your breast, and what husband's heart is not touched, seeing his wife nursing his child! A plump little rosy baby, sprawling and snuggling, with chubby little hands and feet; with clean, tiny little nails, so tiny that it makes one laugh to look at them; with little eyes that look as if he already understands everything. And as he sucks, he clutches at your breast with his little hand and plays. When his father approaches, the child tears itself away from your breast, bends himself back, looks at his father, laughs, as if God only knows how funny it all is — and then he starts sucking again. Or he'll go and bite his mother's breast when his little teeth are cutting through, and then he looks sideways at her with his little eyes as if to say, 'Look, I bit you!' Isn't this perfect happiness, when the three of them — husband, wife, and child — are together? One can forgive a great deal for the sake of such moments. Yes, Liza, one must first learn to live oneself before one blames others!"

"So, I can use these vignettes, these little vignettes, to get to you," I thought to myself, although, honest to God, I spoke with real feeling, and suddenly I blushed. "What if she suddenly bursts out laughing — into what hole will I crawl then?" The idea infuriated me. By the end of my speech I really did get excited, and now my vanity was somehow wounded. The silence continued. I even wanted to push her.

"Why, you . . ." she began suddenly, and stopped.

But I understood everything: there was a quiver of something different in her voice, not abrupt, harsh, and unyielding as before, but something soft and bashful, so bashful that I myself suddenly felt bashful and guilty before her.

"What?" I asked, with tender curiosity.

"Why, you . . ."

"What?"

"Why, you . . . talk as if you were reading from a book," she said, and again there appeared to be a note of sarcasm in her voice.

That remark stung me painfully. It was not what I was expecting.

I didn't understand that she was hiding her feelings behind a mask of sarcasm, that this is usually the last refuge of a bashful and chaste-hearted person whose soul is being rudely and insolently invaded, and who will not surrender until the last minute out of pride, and is afraid of expressing any feeling before you. I should already have guessed the truth from the timidity with which, through a number of intermediary steps, she had approached her sarcasm before she finally decided to express it. But I didn't guess, and an evil feeling took possession of me.

"Just you wait!" I thought.

VII

"Come on, Liza, what kind of book can you be talking about, when even I, an outsider, find all this so repulsive? Even though I don't look at it as an outsider. All this has been awakened in my soul now. . . . Can it be, can it be that you yourself don't find all this repulsive? No, habit clearly means a lot! Hell, habit can change a person beyond recognition. Can you seriously think that you'll never grow old, that you'll remain eternally pretty, and that they'll keep you here forever and ever? I won't even mention how foul it is here. . . . Though, here's what I'll tell you about it — about your present life, I mean: at present, even though you're young, attractive, sympathetic, with a soul, with feeling, do you know that, as soon as I came to a little while ago, I immediately felt disgust at being here with you! A man has to be drunk to wind up here. But if you were in some other place, living as decent people live, I would perhaps not merely be attracted to you but would even fall in love with you, would be glad of a look from you, let alone a word. I'd watch for you by the gate, go down on my knees before you, look upon you as my betrothed, and think it an honor to be allowed to. I wouldn't dare think an impure thought about you. But here, I know I just have to whistle and, whether you like it or not, you have to go with me, and it's no longer I who obey your wishes, but you who obey mine. The lowliest peasant hires himself out as a laborer, but he doesn't sell himself into slavery; besides, he knows that he'll be free again when his term of work ends. But when does your term end? Just think: What are you giving up here? What are you selling into slavery? It's your soul, your soul, which you have no right to dispose of, that you're enslaving together with your body! You give your love to be defiled by every drunkard! Love! But, after all, love is everything; after all, it's a diamond, a maiden's treasure. Why, to become worthy of that love, some men would be ready to give their souls, to face death. But what value is placed on your love now? You've been bought, all of you, and why should one strive to gain love here when one can have everything even without love? And, after all, there's no greater insult for a girl, do you understand? To be sure, I've heard that they indulge you foolish girls — they let you have lovers of your own here. But you know that's simply a farce, a deception; they're laughing at you, and you believe it! Why, do you suppose he really loves you, that lover of yours? I don't believe it. How can he love you when he knows you may be called away from him any minute? He'd be depraved if he did! Does he have a drop of respect for you? What do you have in common with him? He laughs at you and robs you — that's what his love amounts to! You're lucky if he doesn't beat you. But maybe he does. Ask your lover, if you have one, whether he'll marry you. He'll laugh in your face, if he doesn't spit in it or beat you — even though it may be that he's not worth a few lousy pennies himself. And for the sake of what have you ruined your life here, if you come to think of it? For the coffee they give you to drink and the plentiful meals? But why are they feeding you so well? Another girl, an honest one, would choke on every bite, because she'd know why she was being fed. You're in debt here, and, of course, you'll always be in debt, and you'll go on being in debt to the end, until such time comes as the customers begin to spurn you. And that'll happen soon; don't rely on your youth. Everything here flies by like a fast coach. You'll be kicked out. And not simply kicked out; long before that they'll start picking on you, reproaching you, cursing at you — as if it wasn't you who had sacrificed your health for the madam, ruined your youth and your soul in vain for her benefit, but rather as if it were you who had ruined her, turned her out into the world, robbed her. And don't expect anyone to take your part: the others, your friends, will attack you, too, in order to win her favor, because everyone here is a slave and lost all conscience and pity long ago. They've become utterly vile, and nothing on earth is viler, more loathsome, or more insulting than this abuse. Nevertheless, you'll sacrifice everything here, everything without exception — your health and your youth and your beauty and your hopes; and at twenty-two you'll look like a woman of thirty-five, and you'll be lucky if you're not diseased — pray to God to keep you from that! No doubt you're thinking now that you're not really working, that it's all a stroll in the park! Yet there's no work in the world that's harder and more back-breaking, and there never has been. You'd think that the heart alone would be worn out with tears. And you won't dare say a word, not half a word, when they drive you away from here; you'll go away as though you were to blame. You'll go to another house, then to a third, then somewhere else, till you end up in the Haymarket. There you'll be beaten at every opportunity; that's what passes for courtesy there: the customer's way of caressing you is first to beat you senseless. You don't believe that it's so revolting there? Go and look for yourself sometime; you can see it with your own eyes. Once, one New Year's Day, I saw a woman outside the door there, alone. Her own friends had thrown her out for the fun of it, to freeze her a little bit, because she'd been howling too much, and they'd locked the door behind her. At nine in the morning she was already completely drunk; she was disheveled, half-naked, and all beaten up. Her face was powdered, but her eyes were black and blue; blood was trickling from her nose and her teeth; some cabby had just given her a beating. She was sitting on the stone steps, holding some sort of salted fish; she was howling and chanting something about her 'dest-ny,' and banging the fish on the steps. Meanwhile, cabbies and drunken soldiers had crowded around her and were taunting her. You don't believe that you'll ever be like that? I wouldn't like to believe it, either, but how do you know? Maybe ten years, eight years ago that very woman with the salted fish had come here fresh as a little cherub, innocent, pure, knowing no evil, blushing at every word. Perhaps she was the way you are now, proud, easily offended, not resembling the others; perhaps she looked like a queen, and knew that everlasting happiness awaited the man who would love her and whom she would love. Do you see how it ended? And what if at that very moment when, drunk and disheveled, she was banging on the filthy steps with that fish — what if at that very moment she was recalling all her former pure years in her father's house, when she used to go to school and the neighbor's son would watch for her on the way, assuring her that he'd love her all his life, that he'd devote his life to her, and when they vowed to love each other forever and be married as soon as they were grown up! No, Liza, happiness, happiness for you would be to die of consumption as soon as possible in some corner, in some cellar, like the woman I just told you about. The hospital, you say? You'll be lucky if they take you, but what if you're still of use to the madam? Consumption is a queer sickness; it's not like fever. You go on hoping till the last minute and keep saying you're healthy. And so you delude yourself. And that suits your madam just fine. Don't trouble yourself — that's how it is; in other words, you've sold your soul, and what's more, you owe money, so you don't dare say a word. And when you're dying, everyone will abandon you, everyone will turn away — because what can they take from you then? What's more, they'll reproach you for taking up space for free, for taking so long to die. However you beg, you won't get as much as a drink of water without abuse: 'When are you going to croak, you bitch? You keep us awake with your moaning; the gentlemen are disgusted.' That's true; I've overheard such words myself. When you're dying, they'll shove you into the filthiest corner in the cellar — into the darkness and dampness; what will your thoughts be when you're lying there alone? And when you die, strangers will lay you out in a hurry, with grumbling and impatience; no one will bless you, no one will sigh for you — they'll only want to get rid of you as soon as possible. They'll buy a

93

cheap pine box, carry you out as they did that poor woman today, and go to the tavern to celebrate your memory. There'll be slush, filth, wet snow in the grave — why should they put themselves out for you? 'Lower her down, Vanyukha; it must be her "dest'ny": even here, she's going down with her legs up, the bitch. Shorten the rope, you jerk.' 'It's all right as it is.' 'What's all right? She's lying on her side! She was a human being too, wasn't she? Well, all right, let's cover her up.' And they won't spend a lot of time arguing over you. They'll cover you with the wet blue clay as quick as they can and go off to the tavern. . . . And that's the end of your memory on earth; other women's graves are visited by their children, their fathers, their husbands, but for you there are no tears, no sighs, no remembrance; and no one, no one in the whole world, will ever come to see you; your name will vanish from the face of the earth — as if you had never existed, as if you had never been born at all! Mud and swamp; nothing left to do but knock on your coffin lid at night, when the dead rise: 'Let me out, good people, to live in the world! I lived, but didn't see life; my life was thrown away like an old rag; it was drunk away in a tavern on the Haymarket; let me out, good people, to live in the world one more time.'"

And I worked myself up to such a pitch of feeling that I began to feel a lump forming in my throat, and . . . suddenly I stopped, rose up in alarm, and, inclining my head apprehensively, began to listen with a pounding heart. There was indeed cause for dismay.

For a long time already I'd felt that I had turned Liza's soul upside down and broken her heart; and the more I became convinced of this, the more I desired to attain my goal as quickly and forcefully as possible. The game, the game carried me away; yet it wasn't just the game. . . .

I knew I'd been speaking stiffly, artificially, even bookishly; in short, I didn't know how to speak except "like a book." But that didn't trouble me; I knew, I felt that I'd be understood, and that this very bookishness might even help me in my task. But now, having attained my effect, I suddenly lost my nerve. No, never, never before had I witnessed such despair! She was lying prone, her face pressed deep into a pillow which she was clutching with her hands. Her chest heaved uncontrollably. Her young body was shuddering all over, as if in convulsions. Her sobs, suppressed within her breast, would suddenly burst out in wailing and cries and would tear her apart. Then she'd cling to the pillow even more tightly: she didn't want anyone here, not a single living soul, to learn of her anguish and tears. She bit the pillow, she bit her own hand until it bled (I saw that afterwards), and, clutching her loosened braids, she grew rigid with this exertion, holding her breath and clenching her teeth. I began saying something, begging her to calm herself, but felt that I didn't dare; and suddenly, in a sort of cold shiver, almost in a panic, I started groping hurriedly for my things, in a helter-skelter effort to get out of there. It was dark; however I tried, I couldn't get myself together. Suddenly I felt a box of matches and a candlestick with a whole candle in it. As soon as the room was illuminated, Liza suddenly jumped up, then sat down, and looked at me almost senselessly, with a contorted face and a half-crazed smile. I sat down beside her and took her hands; she came to herself, threw herself toward me as if to embrace me, but didn't dare, and gently inclined her head before me.

"Liza, my friend, I didn't mean it . . . forgive me," I began, but she squeezed my hands with such force that I realized I was saying the wrong thing, and I stopped.

"Here's my address, Liza. Come see me."

"I'll come . . ." she whispered resolutely, still not raising her head.

"But I'm leaving now. Farewell . . . till we meet again."

I stood up; she did too, and suddenly blushed all over, shuddered, grabbed a shawl that was lying on a chair, and threw it over her shoulders, wrapping herself up to her chin. Having done this, she again smiled in a sort of sickly way, blushed, and looked at me strangely. I felt pained; I was in a hurry to leave, to vanish.

"Wait a moment," she said suddenly, when we were already in the hallway at the door, stopping me by grabbing hold of my overcoat, and she hurriedly put down the candle and ran off — evidently she had remembered something or wanted to show me something. As she ran off, she was blushing all over, her eyes were gleaming, and a smile appeared on her lips — what did this mean? Against my will I waited; she returned in a minute, and she looked at me as if she wanted to ask forgiveness for something. It wasn't the same face, it wasn't the same look as before — sullen, mistrustful, and obstinate. Her look now was imploring, soft, and at the same time trusting, tender, timid. This is how children look at people whom they love very much and of whom they are asking something. Her eyes were light brown, beautiful eyes, full of life, capable of expressing love as well as sullen hatred.

Without explaining anything to me, as if I were some sort of higher being who was supposed to know everything without explanation, she held out a piece of paper to me. At that moment her whole face was positively shining with the most naïve, almost childlike triumph. I unfolded the paper. It was a letter to her from a medical student or someone of that sort — a very high-flown, flowery, but extremely respectful declaration of love. I don't recall the expressions used, but I remember very well that, behind the high-flown phrases, one could clearly discern a genuine feeling, something which can't be faked. When I'd finished reading it, I met her ardent, questioning, and childishly impatient eyes fixed upon me. She fastened her eyes upon my face and waited impatiently for what I would say. In a few words, hurriedly, but with a sort of joy and pride, she explained to me that she had been to a dance at the house of "very, very good people, *family people*, where *they still know nothing*, absolutely nothing," because she's still quite new here (in this place of our encounter) and is here almost by accident . . . and hasn't yet decided whether she'll stay and will certainly leave as soon as she has paid off her debt. . . . "So, this student was there; he danced with me all evening and talked to me, and it turned out that he had known me long ago in Riga when he was a child; we had played together, but a very long time ago — and he knows my parents, but *about this* he knows nothing, nothing, nothing, and he suspects nothing! And so the day after the dance (three days ago), he sent me this letter through the girlfriend I went to the party with . . . and . . . well, that's the whole story."

She lowered her glittering eyes somewhat shyly when she finished.

Poor girl, she was keeping that student's letter like a precious treasure, and had run to get it, her only treasure, not wanting me to leave without learning that she, too, was honorably and truly loved, that she, too, was spoken to respectfully. No doubt that letter was destined to lie in a box and come to nothing. But it didn't matter: I was certain she would keep it her whole life as a precious treasure, as her pride and justification, and now, at such a moment, she remembered that letter and brought it out to boast naïvely in front of me, to raise herself in my eyes, so that I, too, might see, so that I, too, might praise. I said nothing, pressed her hand, and went out. You don't know how much I wanted to leave. . . . I walked all the way home, despite the fact that the wet snow was still falling in thick flakes. I was exhausted, oppressed, bewildered. But the truth was already shining through my bewilderment. A vile truth!

VIII

However, it was some time before I agreed to acknowledge that truth. Waking up in the morning after several hours of heavy, leaden sleep, and immediately remembering all that had happened the previous day, I was even amazed at my *sentimentality* with Liza, at all that "horror and pity." "To think I had such an attack of womanish hysteria!" I concluded. "And why did I give her my address? What if she comes? Let her come, though; it doesn't matter. . . ." But, *obviously*, that was not the most important matter now: I had to hurry and, whatever the cost, save my reputation in the eyes of Zverkov and Simonov as quickly as possible. That was the most important matter. And I was so busy that morning that I forgot all about Liza.

First of all, I had to repay immediately what I'd borrowed yesterday from Simonov. I decided on a desperate measure: to borrow fifteen roubles from Anton Antonovich. As if on purpose he was in the best of moods that morning, and gave me the money at once, at my first request. I was so delighted at this that, as I signed the receipt with a kind of swaggering air, I informed him *casually* that yesterday "I had been carousing with some friends at the Hôtel de Paris; we were throwing a farewell party for a comrade — in fact, I might say a friend of my childhood — and you know, he's quite a carouser, terribly spoiled, but of course, he belongs to a good family, and has considerable means, a brilliant career; he's witty, charming, a regular Don Juan with the ladies, you understand; we drank an extra 'half-dozen' and. . . ." And it went off all right: all of it was uttered very lightly, freely, and smugly.

When I came home, I immediately wrote to Simonov.

To this day I can't help admiring the truly gentlemanly, good-natured, candid tone of my letter. Adroitly and nobly, and, above all, entirely without any superfluous words, I blamed myself for all that had happened. I justified myself, "if it is at all permissible for me to justify myself," by saying that, being utterly unaccustomed to wine, I had become intoxicated with the first glass, which I had (supposedly) drunk before they arrived as I was waiting for them in the Hôtel de Paris between five and six. I especially begged Simonov's pardon; I asked him to convey my explanation to all the others, and especially to Zverkov, whom — "I remember this as if in a dream" — I evidently had insulted. I added that I would have personally called upon all of them but that my head ached and — this was the main reason — I was embarrassed. I was particularly pleased with a "certain lightness," almost carelessness (strictly within the bounds of politeness, however), which was apparent in my style, and better than any possible arguments gave them to understand at once that I took a rather independent view of "all that unpleasantness last night"; that I was by no means so utterly crushed as you, gentlemen, probably think, but on the contrary, looked upon it as befits a gentleman who serenely respects himself. "No reproach is cast on a young blade's past," as they say.

"There's even an aristocratic playfulness about it!" I thought admiringly as I reread the letter. "And it's all because I'm a cultivated and educated man! Another man in my place wouldn't have known how to extricate himself, but here I've managed to wriggle out of it and am as merry as ever, and all because I'm 'an educated and cultivated man of our time.' And, indeed, perhaps everything really was due to the wine yesterday. Hmm . . . no, it wasn't the wine. I didn't drink any vodka at all between five and six when I was waiting for them. I lied to Simonov; I lied shamelessly; and even now I'm not ashamed. . . .

"Anyway, time to spit on it! I've wriggled out of it — that's the main thing."

I put six roubles in the letter, sealed it, and asked Apollon to take it to Simonov. When he learned there was money in the letter, Apollon became more respectful and agreed to take it. As evening approached, I went out for a walk. My head was still aching and spinning after yesterday. But the more the evening advanced and the twilight thickened, the more changeable and confused my impressions, and consequently my thoughts, became. Something deep inside me, in the depths of my heart and conscience, wouldn't die, didn't want to die, and expressed itself in acute anguish. I wandered mainly along the most crowded commercial streets, along Meshchanskaya, Sadovaya, near the Yusupov Garden. I always loved strolling along these streets at twilight, when they'd become crowded with all sorts of pedestrians, merchants, and tradesmen going home from their daily work, their faces preoccupied to the point of anger. What I liked was that cheap bustle, that insolent prose of life. But on this occasion the jostling of the streets irritated me more than ever. I couldn't figure out what was wrong with me; I didn't have a clue. Something was rising, rising up in my soul, incessantly, painfully, and it refused to be still. I returned home completely upset. It was as if some crime were weighing on my soul.

I was constantly tortured by the thought that Liza might come to see me. It seemed strange to me that, of all of yesterday's memories, it was the memory of her that tortured me in some special way, somehow quite separately. By evening I had succeeded in forgetting about everything else; I had dismissed it all and was still perfectly satisfied with my letter to Simonov. But on this point I somehow wasn't satisfied. It was as if I was tormented only by Liza. "What if she comes?" I thought incessantly. "Well, it doesn't matter — let her come! Hmm. It's bad, though, that she'll see, for instance, how I live. Yesterday I showed myself off as such a . . . hero before her . . . whereas now, hmm! It's bad, though, that I've let myself go to such an extent. Such squalor in my apartment. How did I dare go to dinner yesterday in such clothes! And this oil-cloth sofa of mine with the stuffing sticking out! And my dressing gown, which doesn't cover me! It's nothing but rags. . . . And she'll see it all, and she'll see Apollon. That beast is certain to insult her. He'll pick on her just to be rude to me. And of course, as is my habit, I'll be a coward:

99

I'll start bowing and scraping in front of her and pulling my dressing gown around me; I'll start smiling; I'll start lying. Oh, vileness! But that isn't even the main vileness! There's something more important here, more disgusting and more foul! Yes, more foul! And again and again to put on that dishonest, lying mask! . . ."

When I reached that thought, I flared up in anger:

"Why dishonest? How dishonest? I was speaking sincerely yesterday. I remember there was real feeling in me, too. What I wanted was to arouse noble feelings in her. . . . If she was crying, it was a good thing; it'll have a good effect."

Nevertheless, I couldn't calm down.

All that evening, after I had returned home, even after nine o'clock, when by my calculations Liza couldn't possibly come, she was still haunting my thoughts, and — this is the main thing — I always remembered her in the same position. Of all that had happened yesterday, I pictured one moment with particular vividness: it was when I struck a match to illuminate the room and saw her pale, contorted face with its tortured look. And what a pitiful, what an unnatural, what a contorted smile she was wearing at that moment! But I didn't know then that even fifteen years later I'd still be picturing Liza to myself with the pitiful, contorted, pointless smile she was wearing at that moment.

The next day I was again prepared to regard it all as nonsense, due to over-excited nerves, and, above all, as *exaggerated*. I was always conscious of that weak point of mine, and was sometimes very much afraid of it: "I exaggerate everything — that's where I go wrong," I repeated to myself every hour. But nevertheless, "nevertheless, Liza may still come" — that was the refrain with which all my reflections ended. I was so agitated that I sometimes flew into a fury: "She'll come — she's certain to come!" I'd exclaim, running about the room. "If not today, she'll come tomorrow; she'll find me! That's the damned romanticism of all these *pure hearts!* Oh, the vileness, oh, the stupidity, oh, the narrowness of these 'rotten, sentimental souls'! How can one not understand — really, how can one not understand?" But here I'd stop, and my confusion would be even more profound.

"And how few, how few words were needed," I thought in passing, "how little of the idyllic (and of the affectedly, bookishly, artificially idyllic, too) was needed to immediately turn a whole human soul the way I wanted. That's real virginity! Real virgin soil!"

At times the thought entered my head that I should go see her, "to tell her everything" and prevail on her not to come to me. But this thought provoked such rage in me that I might have crushed that "damned" Liza if she'd suddenly turned up next to me. I would have insulted her, spat at her, kicked her out, hit her!

One day passed, however, and then another and another; she didn't come, and I began to grow calmer. I'd feel particularly bold and let myself go after nine o'clock; sometimes I'd even begin to dream, and rather sweetly: For example, I save Liza precisely by the fact that she comes to see me and I talk to her. . . . I mold her, educate her. Finally, I notice that she loves me, loves me passionately. I pretend not to understand (I don't know, however, why I pretend; just for the beauty of it, I suppose). Finally, embarrassed, beautiful, she throws herself trembling and sobbing at my feet and tells me that I'm her savior and that she loves me more than anything in the world. I'm astonished, but . . . I say, "Liza, do you really think I haven't noticed your love for me? I saw everything, I guessed, but I didn't dare to intrude on your heart first, because I had an influence over you and was afraid that you'd deliberately compel yourself to return my love out of gratitude, that you'd force yourself to feel something for me that perhaps doesn't exist, and I didn't want that because that's . . . despotism. . . . It's indelicate [well, in short, here I launched into some sort of European, George-Sandian,[21] inexplicably noble subtleties]. But now, now you're mine, you're my creation, you're pure, beautiful — you're my beautiful wife."

Into my house come bold and free,
Its rightful mistress there to be.[22]

---

21. In the mid-nineteenth century, the French novelist George Sand (1804-1876) was admired for her "lofty" concerns, ranging from romantic love to social reform. *Trans.*

22. These are the concluding lines of Nekrasov's poem "When from dark error's subjugation," quoted as the epigraph to Part Two of this book. *Trans.*

"Then we would begin to live happily ever after, to travel abroad, etc., etc." In short, all this would begin to nauseate even me, and I'd conclude by sticking my tongue out at myself.

"Besides, they won't let her out, 'the miserable bitch!' " I thought. "I don't think they let them go out very readily, especially in the evening [for some reason it seemed certain to me that she'd come in the evening, and precisely at seven o'clock]. Although she did say she wasn't altogether a slave there yet, that she had certain rights; that means — hmm! Damn it all, she'll come — she's sure to come!"

It was a good thing that Apollon distracted me at that time with his rudeness. He made me lose all patience! He was the bane of my existence, a scourge sent down upon me by Providence. We'd been squabbling constantly for years now, and I hated him. God, how I hated him! I think I've never hated anyone in my life as much as I hated him, particularly at certain moments. He was an elderly, dignified man who worked part of his time as a tailor. But for some unknown reason he despised me beyond all measure, and he looked down upon me insufferably. Although, to be sure, he looked down upon everyone. One glance at that flaxen, smoothly brushed head, at the tuft of hair he curled up on his forehead and greased with vegetable oil, at that dignified mouth, always pursed into the shape of the letter V, and you immediately felt you were in the presence of a being who never doubted himself. He was a pedant of the highest order and the greatest pedant I've ever met on earth, and with that he had a vanity perhaps befitting only Alexander of Macedon. He was in love with every button on his coat, with every one of his fingernails — absolutely in love with them, and he looked it! He treated me quite tyrannically and spoke very little to me, and if he chanced to glance at me, he did so with a firm, majestically self-confident, and invariably mocking look that sometimes drove me into a rage. He fulfilled his duties with the air of doing me the greatest favor. However, he did almost nothing at all for me, and didn't even consider himself obligated to do anything. There can be no doubt that he considered me the greatest fool on earth and that if "he kept me on," it was solely because he could receive his wages from me every month. He consented to "do nothing" for me for seven roubles a month. Many sins will be forgiven me for what I suffered from him. My hatred sometimes reached such a point that simply his manner of walking would nearly throw me into convulsions. But what I loathed particularly was his lisp. His tongue must have been somewhat longer than normal, or something of that sort, because he was constantly lisping and hissing, and he seemed to be awfully proud of this, imagining that it greatly added to his dignity. He spoke softly, in a measured way, with his hands behind his back and his eyes fixed on the ground. He'd particularly madden me when he'd read the Psalter aloud to himself behind his partition. I waged many a battle over that reading. But he was awfully fond of reading aloud in the evenings, in a soft, even, singsong voice, as though over the dead. It's curious that that's how he ended up: at the present time, he hires himself out to read the Psalter over the dead; in addition, he exterminates rats and makes shoe polish. But at that time I couldn't get rid of him; it was as though he was chemically fused with my existence. Besides, he himself would never have agreed to leave me for anything. I couldn't live in *chambres garnies:*[23] my apartment was my solitary refuge, my shell, my lair, in which I concealed myself from all humankind, and Apollon seemed to me — the devil knows why — an integral part of that apartment, and for seven long years I couldn't kick him out.

To be two or three days behind with his wages, for example, was impossible. He'd make such a fuss that I wouldn't know where to hide. But in those days I was so embittered toward everyone that, for some reason and with some purpose in mind, I decided to *punish* Apollon by not paying him his wages for another two weeks. I'd been intending to do this for a long time now, for two years or so, solely in order to prove to him that he dare not treat me in such a superior manner, and that if I wanted to, I could always withhold his wages. It was my plan to say nothing to him about this, and even to be silent on purpose, in order to defeat his pride and force him to be the first to speak of his wages. Then I'd take the whole seven roubles out of a drawer, to show him that I had them and that I had deliberately set them aside, but that I "didn't want,

---

23. *Chambres garnies* (French) are furnished rooms. Living in such quarters would make a servant unnecessary, but would expose the Underground Man to other lodgers. *Trans.*

didn't want, simply didn't want to pay him his wages; I didn't want to because *that's what I wanted,*" because such is "my will as the master," because he's disrespectful, because he's rude; but if he were to ask respectfully, I might be mollified and give him the money; otherwise, he'd have to wait another two weeks, another three weeks, a whole month. . . .

But, angry as I was, he still defeated me. I couldn't even hold out for four days. He began as he always did in such cases, for there had been such cases already, there had been attempts (and let me remark that I knew all this beforehand; I knew his vile tactics by heart) — namely, he'd begin by fixing upon me an exceedingly severe stare, and keeping it up for several minutes at a time, especially on meeting me when I came in or on seeing me out of the house. If, for example, I held out and pretended not to notice these stares, he would, still in silence, proceed to further tortures. Suddenly, apropos of nothing, he'd glide quietly into my room when I was pacing up and down or reading, stand at the door, one hand behind his back and one foot behind the other, and fix me with a stare that was not just severe but utterly contemptuous. If I suddenly asked him what he wanted, he wouldn't answer me, but would continue staring at me persistently for several more seconds; then, pressing his lips together in a particular way, with a highly significant air, he'd slowly turn around and go back to his room. About two hours later he'd suddenly come out again and again appear before me in the same way. It happened that in my fury I wouldn't even ask him what he wanted, but would simply raise my head abruptly and imperiously and begin staring back at him. So we'd stare at each other for about two minutes; finally, he'd turn around in a slow, dignified way and withdraw for another two hours.

If all this was not enough to bring me to my senses and I continued to rebel, he'd suddenly begin to sigh while looking at me; and he'd sigh long and profoundly, as if each sigh measured the full depth of my moral fall; and, of course, it would end with his complete victory: I'd rage and scream, but would still be forced to give in on the main point of the dispute.

This time the usual "severe stare" maneuvers had scarcely begun when I lost my temper and flew at him in a fury. Even without this, I was irritated beyond all measure.

"Stop!" I cried in a frenzy, as he was slowly and silently turning, with one hand behind his back, in order to return to his room. "Stop! Come back! Come back, I tell you!" And I must have roared so unnaturally that he turned around and even began examining me with a certain surprise. However, he persisted in saying nothing, and that infuriated me.

"How dare you enter my room without permission and look at me like that? Answer!"

But after looking at me calmly for half a minute, he began turning around again.

"Stop!" I bellowed, running up to him. "Don't move! There. Answer at once: What did you come in to look at?"

"If you have any order to give me at present, it's my duty to carry it out," he answered, after another silent pause, with a slow, measured lisp, raising his eyebrows and calmly twisting his head from one side to another — all this with horrifying composure.

"That's not what I'm asking you about, you executioner!" I shouted, shaking with fury. "I'll tell you myself, you executioner, why you keep coming here: you see that I don't give you your wages; you're so proud that you don't want to bow down and ask for them, and so you come to punish me, to torment me with your stupid stares, and you don't even s-s-suspect, you executioner, how stupid this is — stupid, stupid, stupid, stupid!"

He began turning around again in silence, but I grabbed him.

"Listen," I shouted at him. "Here's the money, do you see — here it is!" (I took it out of the drawer.) "Here's the whole seven roubles, but you're not getting it, you're not g-g-getting it until you come respectfully with bowed head to beg my forgiveness. Do you hear?"

"That won't happen!" he answered, with some sort of unnatural self-confidence.

"It will happen!" I shouted. "I give you my word of honor, it will happen!"

"And there's nothing for me to beg your pardon for," he continued, as if he hadn't noticed my screams at all. "Besides, you called me an 'executioner,' for which I can always lodge a complaint against you at the police station for insulting me."

"Go ahead! Go lodge a complaint!" I roared. "Go at once, this very minute, this very second! You're an executioner all the same! Executioner! Executioner!" But he merely looked at me, then turned and, not listening to my summoning shouts, glided to his room without looking back.

"If it hadn't been for Liza, none of this would have happened," I decided inwardly. Then, after standing there for a minute, I myself went behind his partition with a dignified and solemn air, though my heart was beating heavily and violently.

"Apollon!" I said softly and with drawn-out emphasis, though I was breathless. "Go at once, without a moment's delay, and get the police officer."

He had meanwhile settled himself at his table, put on his glasses, and taken up some sewing. But, hearing my order, he burst into a guffaw.

"At once — go this minute, go! Go, or else you can't imagine what will happen!"

"You've certainly lost your mind," he observed, without even raising his head, lisping as slowly as ever and continuing to thread his needle. "Whoever heard of a man sending for the police against himself? And as for trying to frighten me — you're upsetting yourself about nothing, because nothing will come of it."

"Go!" I shrieked, clutching him by the shoulder. I felt that I was about to hit him.

And I didn't notice that, at that moment, the door from the hallway quietly and slowly opened and that some figure entered, stopped, and began to look at us in bewilderment. I glanced, grew petrified with shame, and rushed back to my room. There, clutching at my hair with both hands, I leaned my head against the wall and froze in that position.

About two minutes later I heard Apollon's slow footsteps. "There's *some woman* asking for you," he said, looking at me with particular severity; then he moved aside and let Liza in. He didn't want to go away, and scrutinized us mockingly.

"Go away! Go away!" I commanded, having lost all self-possession. At that moment my clock began whirring and wheezing and struck seven.

IX

Into my house come bold and free,
Its rightful mistress there to be.[24]

I stood before her, crushed, overwhelmed, revoltingly embarrassed, and I think I was smiling as I tried with all my might to wrap myself in my tattered old quilted dressing gown — that is, exactly as I had imagined the scene not long before in a fit of depression. After standing over us for a couple of minutes, Apollon went away, but that didn't make things any easier for me. The worst thing, though, was that she, too, suddenly became embarrassed, and in fact much more than I could have expected. At the sight of me, of course.

"Sit down," I said mechanically, and moved a chair for her up to the table, while I sat down on the sofa. She obediently sat down at once and gazed at me wide-eyed, evidently expecting something from me immediately. The naïvete of this expectation drove me into a rage, but I restrained myself.

Here it would have been appropriate not to notice anything, as though everything had been as usual, but instead, she . . . And I dimly felt that she would pay dearly for *all of this.*

"You caught me in a strange situation, Liza," I began, stammering and knowing that this was the wrong way to begin. "No, no, don't imagine anything!" I cried, seeing that she'd suddenly blushed. "I'm not ashamed of my poverty. . . . On the contrary, I look with pride on my poverty. I'm poor but honorable. . . . One can be poor and honorable," I muttered. "However . . . would you like some tea?"

"No . . ." She was about to say something.

24. See note 22 above. *Trans.*

"Wait!"

I jumped up and ran to Apollon. I felt like disappearing somewhere.

"Apollon," I whispered with feverish rapidity, throwing down before him the seven roubles which had remained all the time in my fist. "Here are your wages; see, I'm giving them to you; but for that you have to rescue me: bring me some tea and some biscuits from the restaurant. If you won't go, you'll make me a very unhappy man! You don't know who this woman is. . . . This means — everything! You may be thinking something. . . . But you don't know who this woman is!"

Apollon, who'd already sat down to his work and put on his glasses again, at first silently looked askance at the money without putting down his needle; then, without paying the slightest attention to me or making any answer, he went on busying himself with his needle, which he had not yet threaded. I waited before him for about three minutes, standing with my arms crossed à la Napoleon. My temples were moist with sweat; I was pale, and felt it. But, thank God, he must have been moved to pity, looking at me. Having threaded his needle, he slowly got up, slowly moved back his chair, slowly took off his glasses, slowly counted the money, and finally, after asking me over his shoulder whether he should get a full portion, slowly walked out of the room. As I was returning to Liza, a thought occurred to me on the way: Maybe I should run away just as I was, in my shabby dressing gown, no matter where, and let come what may.

I sat down again. She looked at me uneasily. We were silent for several minutes.

"I'll kill him," I screamed suddenly, striking the table so hard with my fist that the ink spurted out of the inkstand.

"Lord, what's wrong with you!" she cried, shuddering.

"I'll kill him! I'll kill him!" I shrieked, hitting the table in a perfect frenzy, and at the same time with a perfect understanding of how stupid it was to be in such a frenzy.

"You don't know, Liza, what that executioner is to me. He's my executioner. . . . He went out to get some biscuits; he . . ."

And I suddenly burst into tears. It was a hysterical fit. How ashamed I felt in the midst of my sobs; but still I couldn't restrain them.

She was frightened. "What's wrong with you? What's wrong with you?" she cried, fussing about me.

"Water! Get me some water — over there!" I muttered in a faint voice, though I was inwardly conscious that I could have done very well without water and without muttering in a faint voice. But I was *putting on a show*, as they say, in order to save appearances, although my fit was a genuine one.

She gave me the water, looking at me in bewilderment. At that moment Apollon brought in the tea. It suddenly appeared to me that this commonplace, prosaic tea was terribly indecent and paltry after all that had happened, and I blushed. Liza looked at Apollon with positive alarm. He went out without glancing at us.

"Liza, you despise me, don't you?" I asked, looking at her fixedly, trembling with impatience to know what she was thinking.

She became embarrassed, and didn't know what to answer.

"Drink your tea," I muttered angrily. I was angry at myself, but, of course, it was she who would have to pay for it. A horrible anger against her suddenly surged up in my heart; I think I could have killed her. To revenge myself on her, I vowed inwardly not to say one more word to her during the rest of her visit. "She's the cause of it all," I thought.

Our silence had already lasted for five minutes or so. The tea stood on the table; we didn't touch it; I had reached the point where, in order to embarrass her further, I deliberately didn't begin drinking the tea; as for her, it was awkward for her to begin alone. Several times she glanced at me with sad uncertainty. I was stubbornly silent. Of course, I myself was the chief martyr, because I was fully conscious of the entire revolting meanness of my malicious stupidity, and yet at the same time I couldn't restrain myself.

"I want to . . . leave . . . that place . . . once and for all," she began, in order to break the silence in some way, but, poor girl, this was precisely what she shouldn't have started talking about at such a stupid moment to a man who, even without that, was as stupid as I was. Even *my* heart ached with pity for her ineptness and unnecessary straightforwardness. But something hideous immediately stifled all pity in me; it even provoked me more. Let everything in the world perish — I don't care! Another five minutes passed.

"Perhaps I'm in your way," she began timidly, in a barely audible voice, and started to get up.

But as soon as I saw this first impulse of wounded dignity, I positively trembled with spite, and immediately exploded.

"Why did you come here? Tell me that, please," I began, gasping for breath and not even paying attention to the logical order of my words. I wanted to say everything all at once, in one burst; I didn't care how I began.

"Why did you come here? Answer me! Answer me!" I cried, hardly knowing what I was doing. "I'll tell you, my good girl, why you came. You came because I spoke some *words of pity* to you then. So now you've become all tender, and want to hear more 'words of pity.' Well, you may as well know that I was laughing at you then. And I'm laughing at you now. Why are you shuddering? Yes, I was laughing at you! I had been insulted just before, at dinner, by those men who arrived just before me that evening. I came to your house in order to give one of them a beating, an officer; but I didn't succeed, I didn't find him; so, I had to avenge the insult on someone to restore my ego; you turned up, so I vented my spleen on you and laughed at you. I had been humiliated, so I wanted to humiliate; I had been treated like a rag, so I wanted to show my power. . . . That's what it was, and you thought I had come there on purpose to save you. Yes? Is that what you thought? Is that what you thought?"

I knew that she'd perhaps be confused and not understand the details, but I also knew that she'd understand perfectly the essence of what I was saying. That's exactly what happened. She turned white as a handkerchief, wanted to say something, and her lips twisted in pain; but she fell onto a chair as if she'd been cut down by an axe. And all the time afterwards she listened to me with her mouth gaping and her eyes wide open, shuddering with an awful fear. The cynicism, the cynicism of my words crushed her. . . .

"To save you!" I continued, jumping up from my chair and running up and down the room in front of her. "To save you from what? Maybe

I'm worse than you are. Why didn't you throw it back into my face when I was giving you that sermon: 'Why did you come here? To preach us morality?' Power, power was what I wanted then, sport was what I wanted, I wanted your tears, your humiliation, your hysteria — that's what I wanted then! Of course, I couldn't keep it up then, because I'm crap, I got scared, and — the devil knows why — gave you my address, gave it to you because I'm an idiot. Afterwards, even before I got home, I was cursing you to high heaven because of that address. I hated you already because I had lied to you then. Because the only thing that gives me pleasure is to play with words, to dream in my head, but do you know, what I really want? That you should all go to hell! That's what I want! I want peace. Yes, I'd sell the whole world for a penny, right now, as long as I was left in peace. Should the whole world go to hell, or should I go without my tea? I say that the world can go to hell as long as I always get my tea. Did you know that, or not? Well, I know that I'm a bastard, a villain, an egotist, a lazy idler. Here these last three days I've been trembling, terrified at the thought of your coming. And do you know what particularly agitated me these three days? That I had posed as such a hero before you, and now you'd suddenly see me in this tattered dressing gown, beggarly, revolting. I told you just now that I'm not ashamed of my poverty; but you may as well know that I am ashamed of it; I'm more ashamed of it than of anything, more afraid of it than of being found out if I were a thief, because I'm so vain it's as if my skin had been pulled off and the very air hurts me. Can it be that even now you haven't guessed that I'll never forgive you for having found me in this wretched dressing gown, just as I was hurling myself at Apollon like a spiteful little cur? The savior, the former hero, is hurling himself like a mangy, unkempt dog at his lackey, and the lackey's laughing at him! And I'll never forgive you for the tears I couldn't help shedding in front of you just now, like some silly woman put to shame! And what I'm confessing to you now — that too I'll never forgive you! Yes — you, you alone, must answer for it all because you turned up like this, because I'm a bastard, because I'm the vilest, stupidest, most ridiculous, most petty, and most envious of all the worms crawling on the earth, who are not a bit better than I am, but who — the devil knows why —

III

are never embarrassed, whereas I'll always be kicked around by every variety of vermin — that's my nature! And what affair is it of mine that you don't understand a word of this! And what affair, what affair is it of mine whether you perish in that place or not? Don't you understand that, having confessed this in front of you, I'll hate you for being here and listening? After all, a man makes such a confession only once in his lifetime, and even then it is in hysterics! . . . What more do you want? After all this, why are you still hanging around here, tormenting me, not going away?"

But at this point something strange suddenly happened.

I'd become so accustomed to thinking and imagining everything according to books, and to picturing everything in the world to myself just as I had made it up in my dreams beforehand, that at first I didn't even understand this strange occurrence. This is what happened: Liza, insulted and crushed by me, understood a great deal more than I imagined. She understood from all this the first thing a woman always understands if she loves sincerely: that is, she understood that I was unhappy.

The frightened, wounded expression on her face was replaced first by a look of sorrowful astonishment. When I began calling myself a villain and a bastard and my tears started flowing (the whole tirade was accompanied by tears), her entire face was contorted by some sort of spasm. She was on the verge of getting up and stopping me; when I finished, it was not to my screams that she paid attention: "Why are you here? Why don't you go away?" Rather, she paid attention to how very painful it must have been for me to say all this. Besides, she was so crushed, so abject; she regarded herself as infinitely beneath me; how could she feel anger or take offense? She suddenly leapt up from her chair with some sort of irresistible impulse and extended her arms toward me, yearning to come to me, but still timid and not daring to move from her place. . . . At this point my heart was turned upside down. Then all of a sudden she rushed over to me, threw her arms around my neck, and burst into tears. I couldn't restrain myself, either, and I wept as I never had before. . . .

"They won't let me . . . I can't be . . . good!" I barely managed to say;

then I went to the sofa, fell face down, and sobbed for a quarter of an hour in genuine hysterics. She fell down next to me, embraced me, and remained motionless in that embrace.

But the trouble was that the hysterics had to end sometime. And here (I'm writing the revolting truth, after all), lying prone on the sofa with my face thrust into my nasty leather pillow, I began to feel — little by little, from afar, involuntarily but irresistibly — that, after all, it would be awkward now for me to raise my head and look Liza straight in the eye. What was I ashamed of? I don't know, but I was ashamed. It also came into my confused brain that our roles were now completely reversed, that she was now the heroine, and I was exactly the same sort of humiliated and oppressed creature she'd been in front of me that night, four days ago. . . . And all this came into my mind during those few minutes when I was lying prone on the sofa!

My God! Could it be that I was envious of her, then?

I don't know; to this day I can't decide, and at the time, of course, I was even less able to understand it than now. After all, I can't live without domineering and tyrannizing someone. . . . But . . . but, after all, nothing can be explained by reasoning about it, and consequently it's useless to reason.

I mastered myself, however, and raised my head; I had to raise it sooner or later. . . . And to this day I'm convinced that it was just because I was ashamed to look at her that another feeling was suddenly ignited in my heart and burst into flame . . . a feeling of domination and possession. My eyes gleamed with passion, and I gripped her hands tightly. How I hated her and how I was attracted to her at that moment! The one feeling intensified the other. It almost resembled an act of vengeance! . . . At first her face expressed something like perplexity, or even fear, but only for an instant. She embraced me ecstatically and ardently.

X

A quarter of an hour later I was running up and down the room in furious impatience; every other minute I'd go up to the partition to peer at

Liza through the crack. She was sitting on the floor with her head leaning against the bed, and she must have been crying. But she didn't leave, and that's what irritated me. This time she knew everything. I had insulted her with finality, but . . . there's no need to tell about it. She had figured out that my outburst of passion had been precisely revenge, a new humiliation for her, and that to my earlier, almost objectless hatred there was now added a *personal, envious hatred* of her. . . . I don't maintain, however, that she understood all this clearly; but she certainly did fully understand that I was a loathsome man, and, what was worse, that I was incapable of loving her.

I know some will tell me that all this is improbable — that it's improbable that anyone could be as evil and as stupid as I; they might even add that it's improbable that I couldn't come to love her or at least appreciate her love. But why is it improbable? In the first place, I couldn't love her if only because, I repeat, for me to love meant to tyrannize and morally dominate. My entire life I haven't even been able to imagine any other kind of love, and I've reached the point where sometimes I now think that love really consists in the right to tyrannize the beloved object, a right freely given by the latter. In my underground dreams, too, I never imagined love except as a battle; I always began it with hatred and ended it with moral subjugation, and afterwards I could never picture to myself what I would do with the subjugated object. And what is so improbable about all this? After all, I had succeeded in corrupting myself morally to such an extent, in becoming so unaccustomed to "living life," that I actually thought of reproaching her and putting her to shame for having come to me to hear "words of pity," and I didn't even guess that she had come not at all to hear those words, but to love me, because for a woman it's love that constitutes all resurrection, all salvation from any sort of perdition, and all rebirth; and such resurrection and rebirth can't manifest themselves except in love. However, I didn't hate her all that much when I was running around the room and peeping through the crack in the partition. I was only unbearably oppressed by the fact that she was here. I wanted her to disappear. "Peace" was what I desired; I desired to be left alone in the underground. Because I was unaccustomed to it, "living life" oppressed me to the point where I had trouble breathing.

But several more minutes passed and she still didn't get up, as if she were in a daze of forgetfulness. I was shameless enough to tap lightly at the partition to remind her. . . . She suddenly roused herself, sprang up, and rushed about looking for her shawl, her hat, her fur, as if hurrying somewhere to save herself from me. . . . Two minutes later she slowly came out from behind the partition and looked at me with heavy eyes. I laughed spitefully, though in a forced manner, to *keep up appearances,* and turned away from her gaze.

"Farewell," she said, going toward the door.

I suddenly ran up to her, grabbed her hand, opened it, put something in it . . . and closed it again. Then I immediately turned and quickly sprang away to the opposite corner of the room, so that I wouldn't be able to see . . .

I was just about to lie — to write that I'd done this accidentally, without knowing what I was doing, in complete confusion, through sheer idiocy. But I don't want to lie, and so I'll say straight out that I opened her hand and put money in it . . . because I'm evil. It came into my head to do this while I was running up and down the room and she was sitting behind the partition. But here's what I can say for certain: although I did that cruel thing on purpose, it came not from my heart, but from my evil mind. This cruelty was so contrived, so intentionally invented, so completely a product of the mind, of books, that I myself couldn't endure it even for a moment: first I sprang into the corner in order not to see, and then in shame and despair I rushed after Liza. I opened the door into the hallway and began to listen.

"Liza! Liza!" I called down the stairs, but timidly, in a low voice.

There was no answer, but I thought I heard her footsteps at the bottom of the stairs.

"Liza!" I called, more loudly.

No answer. But at that moment I heard the tight outer glass door to the street open heavily with a creak and slam loudly shut. The sound echoed up the stairs.

She had left. I returned to my room deep in thought. I felt terribly oppressed.

I stopped at the table beside the chair on which she had sat and looked aimlessly before me. A minute passed, and suddenly I shuddered: directly before me on the table I saw . . . in short, I saw a crumpled blue five-rouble note, the very one I had pressed into her hand a minute before. It was the *same* note; it couldn't be another one; there wasn't another one in the apartment. She must have managed to throw it on the table at the exact moment that I was springing into the corner.

Well! I might have expected her to do that. Should I have expected that? No. I was such an egotist, I was so lacking in respect for people, that I couldn't even imagine that she'd do something like that. This was more than I could bear. An instant later I was rushing like a crazy person to get dressed, throwing clothes on haphazardly, and I ran headlong out of the house after her. She couldn't have gotten two hundred paces away when I ran out into the street.

It was quiet; the snow was coming down heavily, falling almost perpendicularly, covering the sidewalk and the deserted street as if with a pillow. There were no passersby; no sound could be heard. The streetlamps glimmered morosely and uselessly. I ran about two hundred paces to the crossroads and stopped.

"Where did she go? And why am I running after her? Why? To fall down before her, to weep with repentance, to kiss her feet, to implore her forgiveness!" I longed for that; my whole breast was being torn to pieces, and never, never will I recall this moment with indifference. "But — why?" I thought. "Wouldn't I hate her, perhaps as soon as tomorrow, just because I had kissed her feet today? Would I bring her happiness? Haven't I found out today once again, for the hundredth time, what my true worth is? Wouldn't I torment her to death?"

I stood in the snow, gazing into the confused darkness, and thought about this.

"And wouldn't it be better, wouldn't it be better?" I fantasized afterwards, at home, stifling the sharp ache of my heart with fantasies. "Wouldn't it be better if she bears the imprint of this insult forever? Insult, after all, is purification; it's the most caustic and painful consciousness! Tomorrow I would have dirtied her soul with myself and made her heart weary. But the insult will never die in her, and however foul the dirt awaiting her, the insult will elevate and purify her . . . by hatred . . .

hmm . . . perhaps, too, by forgiveness. . . . But will all that make things easier for her?" And now, in fact, I'll pose an idle question on my own account: What's better — cheap happiness or elevated suffering? Tell me — what's better?

Those were my reveries as I sat at home that evening, barely alive because of the pain in my soul. I'd never before endured such suffering and repentance; but could there have been the slightest doubt when I ran out from my lodging that I'd turn back after only going halfway? I never met Liza again and never heard anything further about her. I will add, too, that for a long time I remained pleased with the *phrase* about the usefulness of insult and hatred, in spite of the fact that I myself almost became sick with anguish then.

Even now, after so many years, all this is somehow a very *bad* memory for me. I have many bad memories now, but . . . shouldn't I end my "Notes" here? I think it was a mistake to begin writing them. At any rate, I've been feeling ashamed all the time I've been writing this *story;* it's not so much literature as corrective punishment. After all, to tell, for example, long stories about how I've ruined my life through my moral degradation in my corner, through the lack of an appropriate environment, through a divorce from real life, and through vainglorious spite in the underground — this, honest to God, is not interesting; a novel needs a hero, whereas here all the traits for an anti-hero have been assembled *on purpose;* but chiefly, all this produces an awfully unpleasant impression because all of us are divorced from life, all of us limp along, some more, some less. We're so divorced from it that we sometimes feel a sort of revulsion to real "living life," and therefore can't bear to be reminded of it. We've reached a point where we almost regard real "living life" as a labor, as something akin to civil service, and inwardly all of us agree that it's better in books. And why do we mill around sometimes, why are we being so capricious, what are we asking for? We ourselves don't know what. It would be worse for us if our capricious demands were fulfilled. Go on, try — give any one of us, for example, a little more independence, untie our hands, widen the sphere of our activity, relax the supervision over us, and we . . . yes, I assure you, we would at once beg to be taken under supervision again. I know that you might get angry with me for that, and begin shouting and stamping your feet: "Speak for yourself," you'll say, "and about your own miseries in the underground, but don't you dare say *'all of us.'*" Excuse me, gentlemen, but I'm not justifying myself with that "all of us." As for what concerns me in particular, in my life I've only carried to an extreme what you haven't dared to carry even halfway, and what's more, you've mistaken your cowardice for good sense, and thus have found comfort in deceiving yourselves. So that perhaps, after all, I'm more "alive" than you are. Take a closer look at it! After all, we don't even know where life lives now, or what it is, or what it's called. Leave us to ourselves, without our books, and we'll get confused and lose our way at once — we won't know what to attach ourselves to, what to hold on to, what to love and what to hate, what to respect and what to despise. We're even oppressed by having to be human beings — human beings with *our own* real body and blood; we're ashamed of this; we consider it a disgrace and attempt to be some sort of nonexistent universal human beings. We're stillborn, and we've long ceased to be begotten by living fathers, and that pleases us more and more. We're acquiring a taste for it. Soon we'll think up a way to be born from an idea. But enough; I don't want to write any more "from the Underground."

*　　*　　*

However, the "notes" of this paradoxalist do not end here. He couldn't resist, and he kept on writing. But it seems to us, too, that this may be as good a place as any to stop.